"You are now man and wife

in the eyes of God and by the laws of the kingdom. You may kiss your bride, my lord."

Raymond glanced at the man sharply. He didn't want to kiss her. Not here, in the crowded hall, and indeed not ever.

Kissing reminded him too much of Allicia.

"It is to seal the promise, my lord," the priest whispered nervously. "It is not strictly necessary, but the people will be disappointed if you don't."

He didn't care if they were or not.

Suddenly his bride grabbed his shoulders, turned him toward her and heartily bussed him on the lips.

He couldn't have been more surprised if she had drawn a knife and threatened to kill him.

She leaned close. "I want everyone to know I am wed to you of my own free will."

Now *what* could he possibly say to *that?*

Get caught reading Harlequin.

Praise for the recent works of *USA Today* bestselling author Margaret Moore

The Duke's Desire
"This novel is in true Moore style—
sweet, poignant and funny."
—*Halifax Chronicle-Herald*

A Warrior's Kiss
"Margaret Moore remains consistently innovative,
matching an ending of romantic perfection
to the rest of this highly entertaining read."
—*Romantic Times Magazine*

The Welshman's Bride
"This is an exceptional reading experience
for one and all. The warrior series
will touch your heart as few books will."
—*Rendezvous*

THE OVERLORD'S BRIDE
Harlequin Historical #559 May 2001

MARGARET MOORE

THE OVERLORD'S BRIDE

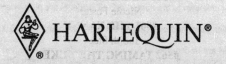

HARLEQUIN®

TORONTO • NEW YORK • LONDON
AMSTERDAM • PARIS • SYDNEY • HAMBURG
STOCKHOLM • ATHENS • TOKYO • MILAN • MADRID
PRAGUE • WARSAW • BUDAPEST • AUCKLAND

ISBN 0-373-29159-0

THE OVERLORD'S BRIDE

Visit us at www.eHarlequin.com

Printed in U.S.A.

Please address questions and book requests to:
Harlequin Reader Service
U.S.: 3010 Walden Ave., P.O. Box 1325, Buffalo, NY 14269
Canadian: P.O. Box 609, Fort Erie, Ont. L2A 5X3

To Tracy Farrell,
who ten years ago made "the call"
that would change my life.

Chapter One

"Stop gawking like a simpleton," Lord Perronet snapped, his hooked nose twitching with annoyance as he waited for his niece's horse to come beside his. "Are you *trying* to look like a fool?"

Elizabeth tore her gaze from the castle ahead. The massive structure loomed out of the gray mist as if it were some sort of angry beast watching its prey come closer. "Given all the unexpected things that have happened to me in the past three days, would it be so surprising if my brains were addled?"

Her uncle's eyes narrowed slightly as he surveyed her with obvious displeasure, as he had at intervals ever since he had come to the convent to take her away. "You're still the same," he muttered. "I was hoping the good sisters had tamed you by now."

"They tried, Uncle, they tried."

He grunted scornfully as he continued his dissatisfied scrutiny.

Elizabeth knew she was not pleasing to look

upon. If she were, she would not have been sent to the holy sisters thirteen years ago, into that horrible living death. She would have stayed with Lady Katherine DuMonde to finish her education in preparation for marriage and her duties as the chatelaine of a castle. She would have married. She would have had children.

"You must make an effort to behave properly, as a highborn lady should," he commanded.

"You wish I were more like my cousin Genevieve, no doubt."

"That harlot? No, I certainly do not."

Elizabeth kept the satisfied smile from her lips. Beautiful, ladylike Genevieve, her cousin, should have been making this journey to Donhallow Castle today. Instead, she had compromised her honor with a Welsh-Norman nobleman and married him, leaving her uncle with a terrible dilemma. He had already arranged a marriage alliance with the powerful Lord Kirkheathe and, rather than have it thwarted, had come to the Convent of the Blessed Sacrament to give Elizabeth the choice of remaining there until the day she died, or taking Genevieve's place as Lord Kirkheathe's bride.

As she had thought then, so she thought now: she had never had a simpler decision to make. A chance for liberty of some sort, or slavery and deprivation for certain.

"You have told me almost nothing of Lord Kirkheathe," Elizabeth prompted as they continued toward Donhallow. Now she could make out a village huddled at the base of its walls, like peasants around a warm fire—a much more pleasing conceit than the first sight of their destination had engendered.

"What is there to know?" her uncle replied. "Kirkheathe is rich, respected, has friends at court and we should pray to heaven he takes you in Genevieve's stead."

"What will happen if he doesn't?"

Her uncle turned his hard black eyes toward her. "Let us just say it will be better if he does. A man needs all the friends at court he can get."

Elizabeth cocked her head to one side. "You do not trust the men at court who are supposed to be your friends?"

Her uncle's face flushed. "I said nothing of the kind."

"Why else seek a family alliance with Lord Kirkheathe? His lands are far from yours."

"Since when has a woman who has spent the past thirteen years in a convent understood anything of politics and alliances?"

"You think there are no politics in a convent? No alliances to be made or broken? No secrets to be kept? No power to crave? By our Lady, Uncle, *I* am not the simpleton if you believe that."

"This is nonsense. All that matters is that Lord Kirkheathe accept you, and then all will be well, for you and for me."

"If I am to confine myself to womanly subjects, Uncle, tell me about the man himself."

"What is there to know beyond what I have told you?"

"Is he handsome?"

Her uncle made a scoffing laugh. "You are hardly in a position to care about the man's looks."

"Since I am no beauty, it has occurred to me that if he is not a fine-looking man, he may care less about my features."

Once more her uncle scrutinized her. "You'd look better without that wimple. Indeed, you resemble Genevieve more than I ever thought possible."

Elizabeth gave him a surprised look. It was impossible that she could look like Genevieve, with her perfect features and beautiful hair. True, Elizabeth had not seen Genevieve since she had left Lady Katherine's care, but still...

"Has Genevieve been ill?" she asked, thinking that perhaps something had happened to ruin Genevieve's looks.

"No. You have improved."

As Elizabeth eyed him skeptically, she recalled every jeer and criticism the other inhabitants of the convent had aimed at her, the Reverend Mother's most of all.

No, she was not pretty. Why even imply that she was? "He doesn't know, does he?"

Her uncle started, making his horse whinny. "Who doesn't know what?"

"Lord Kirkheathe doesn't know about Genevieve, does he?"

"I never said that."

Despite his denial, Elizabeth knew that she had hit the mark. "When do you intend to tell him who I am—before or after the wedding?"

Looking at the road ahead, her uncle didn't respond.

"If he is an important man, you would not be wise to try to trick him. If he has friends at court, he will hear about Genevieve soon enough, and then it would go hard on you, Uncle," Elizabeth said. "Besides, I will not let you. I have no desire to be married under false pretenses."

"Would you rather go back to the convent?"

"No, I would not," she said, meaning it. Life there had been a hell on earth, of near starvation and punishment and toil and cold. "But I will not begin a new life based upon a lie. I have done nothing wrong, and neither have you. Surely he will see that you are trying to keep your bargain. Or was he particular about Genevieve? He cannot have met her, or you would not even think of trying to fool him."

"All Lord Kirkheathe cares about is that his bride be a virgin."

"Well, in that, I am superbly qualified. I hadn't even spoken to a man from the time I arrived at the convent until you came to get me. So, Uncle, I see no need to tell lies. Also, did she not marry into an influential family, too, even if they are Welsh?"

"Welsh with Norman blood," her uncle clarified. "You are right, Elizabeth—so of course I wasn't going to try to pass you off as your cousin."

She didn't believe that for a moment. "Just so long as we understand one another, Uncle."

"I, um, I saw no need to tell him. A Perronet woman is a Perronet woman."

"But I am not Genevieve. I am older than she, for one thing."

"Trust me, Elizabeth."

His words did not comfort her, for she still saw trepidation in his eyes. What if Lord Kirkheathe did not want her? What if he sent her away?

"I would not speak to him as you do to me, Elizabeth," her uncle continued sternly. "I can assure you, a man of his rank and reputation will not stand for it."

"I promise I shall be a very humble and dutiful bride, Uncle," she vowed, determined to do almost anything rather than return to the convent. "The Reverend Mother was very diligent in her efforts to make me humble and dutiful."

"I do not think she succeeded very well."

"She taught me how to look and act humble and dutiful when it is necessary," Elizabeth clarified.

"I wish you would act that way with me."

She gave her uncle a sincere smile. "I have been myself with you, Uncle. Isn't that better?"

"No!"

His harsh response stung her, but she had learned

well how to mask her hurt feelings, too. "How old is Lord Kirkheathe?"

"That doesn't matter either."

"If he is not young, you might want to remember that I could be his widow one day, Uncle. A very rich widow, in charge of a great estate."

Again she hit the target and when he looked at her, there was a hint of grudging respect. "He is, I think, eight and thirty—but you might have a son of age to inherit before he dies."

"I hope we have many sons, and daughters, too. Has he other children?"

"No."

"Has he been married before?"

Her uncle's face reddened as he craned his head to look up at the gray sky. "Enough questions! I think it is going to rain. We had best make haste."

He called an order to the leader of his men, and in the next instant, they were trotting toward the village, and the forbidding castle beyond.

Absently scratching the large head of his hound, Raymond D'Estienne, Lord Kirkheathe, sat upon the chair on the dais in his great hall like a king upon his throne. Around him, a bevy of servants stood waiting, too, tense and expectant, glancing at their lord, each other, or the door to the kitchen. Not a one of them dared to speak, or else they would be looked at by Lord Kirkheathe.

His notice was something they all wished to avoid.

Outside, rain splashed against the thick walls of Donhallow Castle, heavy enough to be audible above the fire crackling in the hearth nearby.

The wedding party was late. Perronet and his niece—and *his* bride—should have been here hours ago, Raymond thought with annoyance.

Perhaps something had delayed them yet again. He had been receiving messengers from Perronet for days, all bearing excuses for his tardiness.

If the man and his niece didn't arrive today, that would be the end of it. He was not a beggar or a fish to be kept dangling on a line. To be sure, he needed the money promised for the girl's dowry, but he could find another bride now that he had finally decided the time had come to marry again. As for the personal attributes of the woman herself, they were far less important than the money she would bring. For the past several years, Raymond had been trying to maintain his castle on the income from his estate, but Donhallow was ancient and in need of more repairs than he could afford without additional income. Rather than let it fall down around him, he would marry.

He also needed a marital alliance, lest his enemy garner more support than he at both the king's court, and that of their common overlord, the earl of Chesney. Perronet and his friends could provide such support.

Raymond's hands balled into fists as they always did when he thought of Fane Montross, his neighbor and enemy.

A cry went up from the wall walk and all the servants glanced nervously at their lord, who made no move at all.

As they had kept him waiting, he would wait here for them. He would not go out in the rain to bid them welcome.

The door to the hall banged open and Barden, the commander of the garrison, marched to a halt, water dripping from his cloak and helmet. "Lord Perronet and his party have come, my lord," he announced.

Raymond inclined his head, and still did not move. Let them understand that he was angry.

Barden, who had begun his career as a foot soldier here, knew better than to wait for more of a response. With the brisk military efficiency he had always possessed, he turned on his heel and departed.

The door opened again a few moments later, and the familiar figure of Lord Perronet hurried into the hall. Behind him, likewise swathed in a dripping cloak, was a woman. The bride, no doubt.

As Raymond watched without any alteration of his expression, Lord Perronet approached and bowed, one wary eye on Raymond's dog, Cadmus. "Forgive us the delay, my lord. The weather has been most unseasonable, as you are no doubt aware, and we had trouble with a lame horse. I cannot possibly say how pleased I am that we have arrived safe at last.''

He made a hopeful smile, which did absolutely nothing to appease Raymond; nevertheless, he finally rose and bowed in response.

''Allow me to present my niece, my lord,'' Perronet said, turning and gesturing for the woman to come forward.

She did, walking neither slowly nor quickly, and as she did, she raised her arms and pushed back the hood of her soaking gray wool cloak.

Perronet had claimed his niece was a great beauty. Raymond had believed that to be a lie, or an exaggeration, something meant to increase the bride's value.

Surprisingly, it was true.

Her slender face was surrounded by the severity of a wimple, but that only seemed to emphasize her lovely features. Large, brown eyes crowned with shapely brows shone in the torchlight. Her nose was perfect, mercifully different from her uncle's, and her cheeks looked as soft as velvet. Then there were her lips, rosy and full, the bottom slightly more than the top. Lips made for kissing.

Pure, raw desire, a sensation last felt so long ago as to be nearly forgotten, hit Raymond, as strong as the blow of an enemy's fist. A need suddenly burned in his blood and sent it throbbing through his body, reminding him of the emptiness of his days. And nights.

Even as these sensations sprang to life, Raymond told himself they were feelings he did not want. The yearning coursing through him was but a weakness—a weakness he had fallen prey to once, and never would again.

The woman came to a halt beside her uncle. She glanced at Perronet, then turned her remarkably intelligent eyes back onto him. "I am Elizabeth Perronet."

Her voice was as unexpected as her face, musical and very pleasant—and very determined. Yet it was not the unexpected nature of her voice that made Raymond frown.

He was supposed to wed Genevieve Perronet.

"My lord," Lord Perronet began placatingly after giving the woman a swift and censorious look. "This is my *other* niece. Genevieve has, um, unfortunately proved herself unworthy of your lordship and the honor of being your bride. Elizabeth, however, is equally suitable—and of course, the dowry remains the same."

Whatever was going on, Raymond realized, they didn't need an audience. They could discuss it in the privacy of the solar. He gestured for Cadmus to stay, then looked pointedly at Lord Perronet before turning toward the tower that held his solar.

The man spoke quietly to his niece. "Wait here. I shall settle this accordingly."

"No, Uncle," she replied, making no effort to speak softly. "This concerns me, so I should be a party to the discussion. I am not a piece of furniture or a block of wood.''

''Elizabeth,'' Perronet warned.

Raymond raised an eyebrow. Lord Perronet instantly started toward him, trailed by his niece.

A bold woman. Was that good—or bad? Allicia had not been bold, not until the last night of her life.

Raymond again started toward the solar and heard them follow.

''Is he mute?'' Elizabeth Perronet whispered as they climbed the tower stairs.

Raymond's lips twisted into a smile as he waited for them at the door to his solar. He let her uncle pass into the room, then, when she was beside him, he answered.

''No, not mute,'' he said in a harsh rasp, all that was left of his once fine voice.

Chapter Two

Elizabeth had never heard anything quite like the soft hoarseness of Lord Kirkheathe's deep voice. It seemed at once intimate and frightening, as if he were part beast and, at the same time, pure human male.

A man might sound like that in the throes of fierce passion, whispering in her ear.

She flushed at that thought, warmth blossoming within her comprised of both shame and excitement. She tried to subdue those emotions, for if ever she needed to keep her wits about her, it was now.

Perhaps he was ill, although he certainly looked healthy. Indeed, he looked extremely fit for a man of eight and thirty, as well as tall, broad-shouldered and imposing, with long, savage hair to his shoulders, iron gray among the thick black. His black tunic, cinched about the waist with a simple leather belt, had swirled about his booted ankles as he strode ahead of her with long, athletic strides.

Sidling in front of him to enter the room, she darted a nervous glance upward and saw the scar around his neck, a mottled, puckered thin red line of flesh.

An injury would explain his voice, yet it was a strange scar, as if he had been hung by his neck with a thin leather band.

She didn't dare look at his face. Was he angry she was not the promised Genevieve? Would he accept her instead, a poor substitute, or would he send her back to the convent?

A single torch in the sconce on the wall lighted the room, but not well enough to reveal the corners. In the center was a large wooden trestle table, as plain as the heavy chair behind it.

Trying not to tremble, Elizabeth waited beside her uncle in an attitude of humility, staring down at the flagstones of the floor.

It might take divine intervention to make her acceptable to this intimidating man with the intimidating dog that was, mercifully, still in the hall.

Please, God, do not let him send me back. Let me stay, she silently prayed. I will be the perfect wife. I will be as humble and demure as I can be. This time, I promise I will. I will do everything I can to be pleasing to my husband—only do not send me back to the Reverend Mother, who detests me and will surely one day punish me to death.

Her uncle shifted nervously. He was more angry than he was afraid. She had seen that in his eyes as he had chastised her; however, one look at Lord Kirkheathe, and she knew she must not lie to him. Not about who she was, or anything else.

Lord Kirkheathe walked around the large table, so it was between them. The oak chair scraped against the floor as he sat.

"My lord," her uncle began in a penitential tone, "you must understand the predicament I was in. Genevieve disgraced us, and yet we had so agreeably decided to join our families. I wondered what I could do, how I could possibly keep my word to you, and then I thought of Elizabeth. I assure you, my lord, she is a virgin. She has been thirteen years in a convent where she never saw or spoke to a man."

"Never?" Lord Kirkheathe asked huskily.

"Never, my lord," she confirmed. "My uncle was the first man I saw in thirteen years."

She raised her eyes, to find his piercing gaze upon her. The torchlight made his face a bronze mask, the hollows beneath his prominent cheekbones dark with shadow.

What did he think of her? Did he see some taint of the deprivations of the convent on her? Did he think her too homely to consider?

He might have been carved from rock, for all she could tell. Then his lips twitched. In a smile? Or was it merely a flicker of the light?

"I know she is not the woman you were promised, my lord," her uncle wheedled, "but she stands in the same relation to me, and the terms of the marriage agreement need not alter.''

"Yes, they should," Elizabeth interjected. She had no idea what the terms of the marriage contract were, but she would not let her uncle's greed rob her of her chance for liberty. "I am not the bride he was promised. That must be taken into account."

"Elizabeth, you forget yourself!"

"No, Uncle, it is you who seems to forget that I am not Genevieve. For whatever reason, Lord Kirkheathe is not getting his promised bride. The dowry should be increased, or some other compensation granted."

"You are not the man's wife yet, by God, to be haggling for him!"

"Uncle, it is only fair—"

"Fair?" he cried, turning on her. "Fair would have been for that slut Genevieve to stay pure and not jump into bed with the first good-looking fellow she could find! Fair would be for you to know your place! Fair would be—"

"Go, Lord Perronet."

The low voice of Lord Kirkheathe cut through the air like a knife. Instantly, her uncle faced him. "Forgive me, my lord," he pleaded. "It has been a long and difficult journey and I fear I lost my temper."

"Leave."

"Perhaps Elizabeth is right, and some suitable increase in the dowry is called for—"

Lord Kirkheathe slowly rose, and her uncle darted out the door.

Confused and uncertain, Elizabeth watched as Lord Kirkheathe resumed his seat. Was this a good sign, or not?

She waited a moment, but when he did not speak, she broke the silence. "Forgive my impertinence in speaking without your leave to my uncle, my lord," she said in what she hoped was a suitably demure and humble voice.

Surprisingly, it was much easier to speak humbly and demurely here than it had ever been when she was with the Reverend Mother. "However, I believe it is right to adjust the dowry."

"Why?"

"Because I am not Genevieve."

"Why?" he repeated.

"Why am I not Genevieve?"

He shook his head. "Why is it right?"

"Because I am not the bride you expected when you made the agreement," she replied. "I am not her equal."

"No?" Now she was certain there was a hint of a smile playing about Lord Kirkheathe's lips.

Was he laughing at her? Did he find her desperation amusing, or the fact that she was homely?

He took a deep breath. "I also want to know why you wish to marry me."

Her brow wrinkled with puzzlement at his request, and sweat trickled down her back as she tried to think of a suitable answer. Her whole future might depend on what she said. "My uncle made an agreement with you. Genevieve is not available, and I am."

He raised his left brow.

"My uncle fears what may happen if he breaks the agreement."

Lord Kirkheathe's brow rose a little more.

"I want to be married, my lord."

The brow fell, and both lowered ominously.

"My lord, if you do not marry me, he will send me back to the convent, and I do not wish to return. It is a miserable life." She approached the table, clasping her hands together like the supplicant she was. "If you marry me, my lord, I promise I shall be a good wife. I shall not complain, or ask for anything."

She colored and fell silent.

"You would ask for something?"

She looked directly into his dark, inscrutable eyes. "I would ask for just one thing, my lord."

He tilted his head questioningly.

"Children. It is the dearest desire of my heart to be a mother."

Another smile, as faint and fleeting as the first.

What she would give to know what he was thinking!

"I know I am not pleasing to the eye," she continued, a note of desperation creeping into her voice, "so if you wish to take a mistress, I shall not fault you for that."

His left brow rose again, and she blushed beneath his steady gaze. "I will keep to my household duties, and never seek to interfere with your governance of the estate."

The brow rose a little higher, and she wracked her brain for other things her former foster mother, Lady Katherine, had told her charges they should do in order to ensure a happily married life. Or if not happy, at least free of conflict.

"I will welcome all your friends and family, and seek to make our home comfortable for them, and you, and any guests."

His expression altered ever so slightly, puzzling her. Did he not want her to be hospitable?

"Fetch your uncle."

Not an acceptance, or a dismissal. Just a command.

She knew there was no reason to hesitate, or to plead. He was a warrior, a commander of men. He had made his decision, and she could not change it.

In that, he was like the Reverend Mother, who had decided upon her arrival at the convent that Elizabeth was trouble in human form, and had never altered that conviction, no matter how Elizabeth had tried.

Hopelessness seized her, yet she could not give up. Not yet. Not without one more effort.

"Please, my lord," she pleaded, "if you accept

me, and unless you are an evil man, I will be the most dutiful and faithful wife a man could wish for.''

He regarded her steadily. "How do you know I am not evil?"

"I don't," she confessed. "Yet I do not think you are, or even in the convent, we would have heard of you. Tales of men's base acts travel faster and better than the good a man may do."

"You have never heard of me?"

"Not until my uncle came to the convent."

She thought he sighed. "Fetch him."

"My lord, please, do not send me back! I would rather die!"

"Or be married to me."

"Yes!"

The moment the word left her lips, she cursed herself for a fool.

What chance had she now as he gestured at the door?

Hopeless, then. She was going back. Back to the frigid quarters and frozen water in the washbasins. Back to the Reverend Mother's colder eye and sharp tongue. Back to the bread she had to pick maggots out of, and thin soup.

So be it, then.

Mustering what dignity she had left, she turned and went to the door, opened it and discovered her uncle pacing outside. "He wishes to see you, Uncle."

His eyes widened hopefully, but she gave him no sign, for good or ill. She glanced back over her shoulder, at the man she did not know, and now would never know. "I shall leave—"

"Stay."

Another command.

If he didn't want her, would he make her stay to hear his rejection from his own lips, in his own harsh voice?

Was she a piece of stone to be ground under his heel? Was she a worm to be trod upon?

Whirling around, she marched back into the room and faced Lord Kirkheathe. She raised her chin defiantly, steeling herself for what was to come.

Barely acknowledging her presence, her uncle hurried to stand before Lord Kirkheathe. "My lord?"

"I will marry her."

He would have her. Dear sweet heavenly Father, he would take her. She did not have to go back.

Elizabeth bowed her head, willing herself to remain on her feet. She had felt faint many times in her life, but that had always been from lack of food and long, sleepless vigils during which she was to contemplate the nature of her terrible sinfulness. Never before had she been dizzy with relief.

And then a pair of strong arms were around her, helping her to a stool she had not noticed in the shadows.

She had not seen a man in thirteen years, and it

had been longer than that since a man had touched her.

Nor had any man ever held her like this, even if it was only to help her.

Clutching Lord Kirkheathe's forearms, her fingers gripped the solid muscle beneath the coarse black wool of his tunic. Her pulse started to race as she inhaled his male scent, so different from the scent of women, or her uncle, with his oriental taste in perfumes.

She wanted to lean her head against his broad chest, to feel even more protected, but she didn't dare.

"Wine?" he asked as he helped her to sit.

"No...yes..."

"Wine, Perronet, there." Lord Kirkheathe pointed into another dim corner, and her uncle fetched a wineskin.

Lord Kirkheathe took it from him and handed it to her.

"Are you ill?"

"No, my lord," she said before she took a drink. She gulped down the cool and excellent wine, then wiped her lips with the back of her hand. She looked up into his angular, unreadable face. "I am happy."

He stepped back as abruptly as if she had spilled the wine on him, then turned on his heel and returned to his seat.

She had spoken too hastily. Again.

Lord Kirkheathe looked at her uncle, then pointed

to one of the dark corners, and Elizabeth saw another chair. Her uncle hurried over and dragged it to the table. "I have the agreement here all ready to be signed, and a duplicate, of course," he said, pulling two rolled documents from within the leather purse attached to his belt. "Now, about the changes to the dowry—"

Elizabeth felt rather than saw Lord Kirkheathe's swift, sharp glance in her direction. "No changes."

She raised her head, but he was not looking at her. He glared at her uncle, who was obviously as puzzled as she.

"Let it be as it was," Lord Kirkheathe said.

"But I am not Genevieve," Elizabeth protested, rising.

"I think Lord Kirkheathe is more than aware of that fact by now," her uncle said through narrowed lips. "I see no need to keep harping on it." He faced Lord Kirkheathe and to her horror, Elizabeth saw greedy speculation dawn upon his face. "The harvest was not as fine as I had hoped this year—"

"When will the wedding be?" she interrupted, determined to put an end to her uncle's attempt to alter the terms in his favor, as was surely his intent. If he angered Lord Kirkheathe—!

"Tomorrow. At the noon."

"Excellent, my lord," Lord Perronet declared. "The sooner the better. No need to wait any longer. And if that horse hadn't gone lame—"

Elizabeth hurried forward. "Why wait until tomorrow? The agreement is here, prepared to be signed. I see no need to wait—unless there is no priest nearby?''

"Donhallow Castle has a priest."

"Well then, my lord, why do we not marry today?''

"Elizabeth, be quiet. You heard Lord Kirkheathe. He has fixed tomorrow for the day and it is not for you to—''

Lord Kirkheathe held up his hand to silence him. For a moment, her uncle stared at his open, callused palm, until Lord Kirkheathe made an impatient gesture indicating he wanted the marriage agreement. ''We will marry today.''

Elizabeth sighed with satisfaction.

Lord Kirkheathe looked up from the document for an instant, yet long enough for their gazes to meet.

He wanted her. She saw it in his dark, mysterious eyes. Because of all she had said, or was there something more? She could not be sure, and yet…and yet she did not doubt that if he did not, there was no power on earth that could have compelled him to accept her.

And she was just as certain that she wanted to feel his arms about her again, to lay her head against him, to have him caress and touch her.

To give her children.

He returned to reading the document, and she let her eyes feast upon him as if he were a painting in the convent chapel. She had had ample time to study the works of art during her many vigils, but none of those works had been as fascinating as Lord Kirkheathe's lean fingers, the sinews taut as bowstrings.

He laid down the first parchment and got to his feet. He went to a cabinet and returned with a clay vessel and a feather. Then, as her uncle chewed his lip in anticipation, he signed his name. With equal deliberation, he read the second, and signed it, too.

Only after all this, did he look at her again. "Come."

"But my lord, the ink is not yet dry."

Lord Kirkheathe ignored her uncle. He held out his hand toward Elizabeth, and with gratitude and hope and not a little trepidation now that the marriage was about to happen, she took it and let him escort her from the room.

Elizabeth hardly knew what to say, if anything, or where to look. At him? Not at him?

She surveyed the stairwell, taking in her surroundings as she had not before. This tower was made of huge stones like the rest of the castle, roughhewn and gray. A handrail had been carved into the stone, and the steps were worn. Donhallow was not newly built, or at least this part of it was of ancient creation.

So full of such thoughts was her mind, she failed to feel a sneeze coming. Too late, she covered her mouth.

"Wet wool always makes me sneeze," she explained as they halted abruptly.

He ran his gaze down her body, still clad in her damp cloak. "Wait here."

He went back, past the solar and up farther into the tower, leaving her on the stairs.

At least he hadn't gone into the solar, to her uncle and the documents. The marriage was going to happen. She didn't have to go back to the convent. Surely whatever marriage might hold, it could not be any worse than what she had already endured.

Her uncle came out the door of the solar, saw her standing alone and hurried toward her. "What in the name of the saints have you done now?" he demanded.

"I sneezed."

"You what?"

"I sneezed, that's all," she repeated. "Wet wool always makes me sneeze. Then Lord Kirkheathe told me to wait here, so I'm waiting—humbly and dutifully," she couldn't resist adding.

"Very amusing, niece," her uncle replied sourly. "You should have been humble and dutiful in the solar. I could have lowered the dowry, I'm sure."

"Or paid more." She cocked her head. "Tell me, Uncle, did you haggle with him over Genevieve?"

He didn't meet her eyes.

"You didn't, did you? He told you the terms, and you agreed because he is not a man you haggle with. It's quite obvious. So why did you think you could bargain with him now? You might have ruined everything."

"Or I might have made better terms."

Elizabeth regarded him skeptically. "Better for you, you mean."

"And you are so wise in the ways of men? You know their sort by sight, do you?"

"I know enough to keep quiet when I should."

Her uncle guffawed. "You, keep quiet? What was all that talk in there, then?" he asked, gesturing at the solar. "God's wounds, woman, you talked plenty enough when you would have done better to keep silent, as befits a mere woman."

"If I had kept silent, I could be riding out the gate this very moment instead of getting married today. I meant, Uncle, that I know when to keep quiet, and when to speak."

"I hope so," he muttered, "or it could go ill for you, even if he seems to want you now."

Elizabeth moved closer to him. "What do you mean?"

"He may not have objected to your boldness today, but he might once you are his wife. You should remember that, Elizabeth. Lord Kirkheathe is not a kindhearted man, and there are things you do not know about him."

She stiffened. "What things?"

Chapter Three

Her uncle's expression grew more guarded. "Nothing to prevent the marriage, I assure you."

"Because you want to be allied with him—is that it?" Elizabeth demanded, wondering if it was possible that she had misread Lord Kirkheathe completely. Perhaps she had been so determined not to return to the convent, she had seen in him what she wanted to see rather than the truth. "Is it that even if he is evil incarnate," she continued, "you would overlook it for the sake of the connection between our families, yet you would generously spare a word of warning to the sacrificial bride?"

"No, no, no!" her uncle protested. "I mean that you have a penchant for annoying people, Elizabeth, and you should not annoy him. You cannot deny that he is not exactly a friendly man. I meant nothing more."

"Yet there is something," she insisted. "I can see it in your face."

"Would you rather go back to the convent?"

She thought of the convent, and the pinched, yet satisfied look that would appear on the Reverend Mother's face if she returned.

Surely she had not been wrong about the man she was to marry. Even in the convent they heard tales of evil men, and Lord Kirkheathe had hastened to her aid when she had been overcome with relief. If he were a cruel or selfish man, he would not have done that.

Nor had he quarreled about the dowry, although he would have been within his rights to do so.

To be sure, he did not appear to be happy, but had she looked any happier to him?

She knew better than to judge solely by outward appearances, too. She had learned that lesson bitterly and well only a few short months after her arrival at the convent, when she had told the pretty and oh-so-agreeable Gertrude of her plan to steal some apples from the nun's pantry. Gertrude had been quick to commend her, and even urged her on—only to go running to tell the Reverend Mother in a bid to gain the woman's approval. The fate of her supposed friend had been far less important to Gertrude.

Had there been a sign of Gertrude's duplicity in her face or expression? Perhaps if Elizabeth had looked harder, or been wiser.

She had looked carefully at Lord Kirkheathe, and

she was wiser. "No, Uncle, I do not wish to return to the convent."

They heard the sound of footsteps on the stairs above, and Lord Kirkheathe appeared, bearing a bundle of dark blue cloth. "A wedding gift," he said, shoving it into her hands. "I will send a servant to take you to my chamber to change. My lord, come with me."

Before Elizabeth could respond, he was already moving down the stairs. Without a word to her, her uncle immediately followed him, leaving Elizabeth alone on the stairs.

She fingered the cloth. It was as soft as a rose petal.

A grim, middle-aged maidservant quickly arrived, slightly out of breath. "I am to show you to my lord's bedchamber."

Elizabeth nodded, then followed the woman upward past the solar.

"This is my lord's bedchamber," the woman said, opening the heavy wooden door at the top of the tower.

Elizabeth entered the chilly room. A single plain oil lamp on a table near the bed provided some extra illumination, and the scent of sheep's tallow hung heavy in the air.

"I'll light the brazier." The woman moved swiftly to take the bundle from Elizabeth. She set it down on the large, equally plain bed made with plain linens and a worn fur coverlet.

"Thank you…?"

"Rual, my lady. My name is Rual."

Elizabeth hesitated a moment, then her curiosity compelled her to continue. "Have you been here in the castle a long time?"

"I came here nigh on ten years ago, my lady."

"Lord Kirkheathe—is he a good master?"

The woman shrugged as she took the lamp toward the brazier near the narrow window and proceeded to light the tinder beneath the coal.

Elizabeth almost wished she hadn't asked. She also remembered Lady Katherine's admonition that a chatelaine should never get too friendly with the servants, lest they lose respect. Despite that advice, Elizabeth wanted to know more. "I would not wish to marry a cruel man."

"Nobody would," Rual answered as she returned the lamp to its place on the table.

It seemed Lord Kirkheathe's servants were as reticent as the man himself. "I saw the scar around his neck. Was he injured? Is that what happened to his voice?"

Rual went to the bed and picked up the bundle. "His throat was crushed," she replied matter-of-factly as she shook out the fabric.

A crushed throat. It sounded horrible, and she was amazed that such a thing had not killed him. But then, he looked to be a very strong and otherwise healthy man. "When did it happen?"

"Before I came, my lady."

"And how...ooooh!" Elizabeth breathed as the bundle proved to be a gown of indigo velvet, the round neck and long cuffs richly embroidered with gold and silver thread.

It was the most beautiful gown she had ever seen. "He has excellent taste."

The maidservant didn't respond as she carefully laid it on the bed.

Did Rual think his taste had failed him in the choice of wife, or that Elizabeth was expecting a compliment? At that thought, Elizabeth very nearly laughed aloud. The day she expected a compliment would be a day of miracles.

But then, she thought as she glanced at the gown upon the bed, perhaps today was indeed such a day.

Rual cleared her throat. "I believe we should not tarry, my lady."

"No, of course not," Elizabeth replied. *Especially since I was the one urging haste.*

She took off her cloak and gave the wet garment to Rual, who laid it over a chair that was as plain as the ones in the solar. Elizabeth removed the scarf and wimple she detested and rubbed her scalp for a moment before running her fingers through her hair to untangle it. Then she took off the plain gown of gray wool, the sort of garment she had been wearing ever since her arrival at the convent. Fortunately, her linen shift was dry enough.

Despite the need to hurry, she approached the gown slowly, reverently, suddenly afraid to touch it, it seemed so rich and fine—too rich and too fine for her.

"Here, my lady, I'll help you," Rual said, holding it up.

Elizabeth stood still as Rual put it over her head and gently tugged it into place. She glanced down, to see the bodice gaping.

"It's a little large," Rual noted, "but I'll pull the laces nice and tight—"

"Not that tight!" Elizabeth gasped as the woman pulled hard. "I can't breathe."

The gown loosened. Marveling still, Elizabeth ran her hands down the bodice, which now gaped only a little, and over the skirt. The fabric was so soft!

"How do you wish to do your hair, my lady?"

"My hair?"

"Braided?" Rual suggested.

Elizabeth considered the loose bodice. Her unbound hair might hide that defect a little. "No, no braids."

"Then I'll comb it." Rual headed toward a small table opposite the bed.

No, no braids, nor scarf or confining wimple, either, Elizabeth thought, and this time, she did laugh.

The maidservant started and looked back at her. "You sound very happy, my lady."

"Why should I not? It is my wedding day."

A little wrinkle appeared between the older woman's eyes, and her expression altered. "Indeed, it is, and aye, we should all be pleased. No doubt our lord craves an heir."

"That is the dearest wish of my heart," Elizabeth answered. She wondered what the maid's guarded expression meant. "Is that so surprising?"

"I thought…"

"What? That I would not wish to do my duty as his wife?"

Rual hesitated before taking up the comb lying on the table. "You do not find him…" She seemed to search for the appropriate word. "Frightening, my lady?"

"Frightening?" To be sure, his voice was unexpected, but if there was anything frightening about Lord Kirkheathe, it was his very presence as much as his voice, Elizabeth decided. "No. Intimidating, perhaps. Does he frighten you?"

"No."

Elizabeth was relieved to hear that.

She noted that the maidservant still had not picked up the comb. "Will he be angry if I use his things?" she asked.

Rual finally took up the comb. "I think not. You're his bride, after all."

Yes, she was his bride, Elizabeth silently concurred, so surely he would not begrudge her the use of a comb.

His dog again at his feet, Raymond sat on the dais of his great hall, his gaze pinned on the shifting shapes of the fire in the hearth. The priest, Father Daniel, stood patiently at his left hand, ready to say the words that would wed him to Elizabeth Perronet. A little farther away, Lord Perronet was slumped over one of the trestle tables already set up for the wedding feast, just as quietly getting drunk on Raymond's wine.

At least it kept him quiet.

Ignoring the bustle of the servants as they put out plate and linen, paying little heed to the delicious smells wafting from the kitchen, Raymond thought back to his other wedding day, nearly twenty years ago. He had been so proud and happy! Allicia had been beautiful, charming, graceful—everything a young man could want in a wife.

He had been too young to see that her beauty and charms were fleeting, and her vanity the only thing likely to last.

Elizabeth Perronet had beauty, aye, yet of a different sort. As lovely as her features were, it was the piercing fire in her eyes, the keen intelligence as she faced him, the determination to be heard, the pride even when she begged him to take her that struck him. No simple creature she, governed by whim and conceit.

Nevertheless, he could not deny that Allicia had other qualities besides form and figure. She had been incredibly loving, until that fateful night when, unusually drowsy, he had felt the bite of leather across his neck, the growing pressure that cut off his breathing, the pain, the blood....

Allicia, dead upon the floor.

Cadmus growled beside him, and it was only then that Raymond realized his hands gripped the arm of his chair so hard, his knuckles were white.

And that his bride stood at the bottom of the tower stairs, waiting as patiently as Father Daniel.

He rose with all the majesty he possessed, and watched her approach.

Her waving chestnut brown hair flowed over her shoulders as if it had a life of its own, the curls catching the light from the candles, torches upon the walls, and the hearth. Yet no light in his hall blazed brighter than her glowing eyes, and the sight of her brilliant smile warmed him more than the burning logs nearby.

He thought of her words in the solar. Did she truly not know how beautiful she was? Had the nuns instilled that much modesty in her? She had certainly sounded sincere enough—about that, and other things.

The gown he had given her looked well on Elizabeth Perronet, too, and gave no hint of its age. He had bought it in London, a gift for Allicia.

He had thought of burning it a hundred times; at present, he was glad he had not. As his hungry gaze traveled down Elizabeth's voluptuous body, the full measure of the perfection of her figure was far more obvious than in that drab gray gown.

Cadmus lumbered to his feet and lifted his head for a pat.

Tearing his gaze away from his bride, Raymond looked down at his faithful hound and reminded himself to trust no one, and no woman most of all, no matter how she smiled or how lovely she looked. He had the ruins of his voice to remind him of that for as long as he lived.

The bride's uncle staggered to his feet, and there was no mistaking the smug triumph on his face.

Raymond told himself he should have demanded that Perronet increase the dowry, instead of being so impressed by his bride. It had been a long time since anyone had dared to argue in front of him. He hadn't realized the energy that sort of disagreement could provoke, especially in a woman. How passionate she had been!

How passionate could she be?

That was unimportant, so long as she gave him an heir. He had no intention of feeling anything for his wife beyond a certain tolerance. As he would trust no woman, he would never love one again, either.

"Have you a ring, my lord?" Father Daniel asked softly.

Raymond took the one that had been his mother's from his little finger and handed it to the priest as Elizabeth came to stand beside him. Father Daniel made the sign of the cross over it, then handed it back.

Raymond turned to face her. He lifted her hand and placed the ring on the fourth finger of her left hand. Without looking at her face, he proceeded to push it slowly downward while Father Daniel intoned, "In the name of the Father, and the Son, and the Holy Ghost, you are now man and wife, in the eyes of God and by the laws of the kingdom. You may kiss your bride, my lord."

Raymond glanced at the man sharply. He didn't want to kiss her. Not here, in the crowded hall, and indeed, not ever.

Kissing reminded him too much of Allicia.

"It is to seal the promise, my lord," the priest whispered nervously. "It is not strictly necessary, but the people will be disappointed if you don't."

He didn't care if they were or not.

Suddenly his bride grabbed his shoulders, turned him toward her and heartily bussed him on the lips.

He couldn't have been more surprised if she had drawn a knife and threatened to kill him.

She leaned close. "I want everyone to know I am wed to you of my own free will."

What could he possibly say to that, except, "Come to the table."

She took his arm again, touching him in a way that felt too much like a caress. "Will you introduce me to your servants and tenants?"

"No."

He didn't look to see if she was upset by that response or not.

As they took their places at the high table, he nodded at Father Daniel.

"Bid welcome to your new chatelaine and mistress of Donhallow Castle, Lady Elizabeth," the priest called out, his voice carrying to the back of the hall as Raymond's could not.

Chapter Four

After Father Daniel blessed the feast, and keeping a wary eye on the huge hound who never strayed far from Lord Kirkheathe's side, Elizabeth sat in the throne-like chair beside her husband and wondered how serious her several errors were. That her husband was angry, she did not doubt. A blind man could feel his cold wrath.

She obviously should not have kissed him, or spoken hastily in response to his shocked visage. And of course, she should have realized that with that husky voice, he might not be able to speak loudly enough to introduce her as the priest had.

Yet she did not regret the kiss, for it was as she had told him: she wanted everybody in the hall to know she wed of her own free will and choice. That way, they would not think to use her against her husband, or try to enlist her aid in their individual causes—something else Lady Katherine had warned against.

By our Lady, she thought as she ran her hand over the fine cloth spread upon the table, enjoying the sensation of the soft linen while surreptitiously watching the man sitting so aloof and still beside her, Lady Katherine had talked about almost everything a wife might need to know except how to deal with a man who didn't speak and had no more expression on his face than an effigy.

Or had she? Hadn't Lady Katherine explained over and over again that it was a wife's duty to please her husband, to mold herself to his desires?

Maybe she would have to be silent, too.

Sweet heaven, she hoped not! Humble and demure she might be able to manage, but silent? She had had enough of keeping quiet. That had been harder for her to bear than the beatings.

The pantler entered with the bread and butter, and the toothsome aroma of hot bread, made of fine flour and browned to perfection, filled her nostrils. Her stomach, so used to the poorest fare, seemed to cry out in approval, growling so loudly, she quickly sucked it in and hoped nobody else heard.

Near her elbow stood a *mazer,* a drinking bowl made of beautifully polished wood and rimmed with silver.

For wine. She would be having wine tonight, and probably good wine, if what she had tasted in the solar and her uncle's slightly inebriated state was any indication of the usual beverage provided by Lord Kirkheathe. Her uncle fancied himself an expert on wines, and if he thought what was offered terrible, he would merely sip as courtesy demanded.

Judging by the color of his nose, he found the wine superb.

Her mouth began to water as a maidservant, young and nervous, set down a perfect loaf of bread before her trencher. As she again breathed in the delectable aroma, she had to fight the urge to grab the entire loaf and bite into it.

And the butter! The butter looked excellent, too, smooth and pale yellow, churned to perfection and molded by a little press into dainty dollops.

But resist the urging of her stomach and her nostrils she must, for she must be dignified now as she had not been before, or who could say what her husband might do to express his wrath? Her uncle had implied that she had best be cautious, something she had forgotten at her wedding.

Nevertheless, she would lunge for the bread soon if Lord Kirkheathe did not break it in a moment, her determination to be careful wilting with the smell of it.

At last he moved, breaking off a piece of the loaf and handing to her. Quickly she took up the knife beside her plate to butter it, then bit into it. It was so good, she closed her eyes in rapture.

"What is it?"

Her eyes flew open.

Lord Kirkheathe regarded her with furrowed brow and serious mien. "You groaned."

"Did I?" she said, feeling the heat of a blush steal over her face. "It's the bread," she explained, holding her piece a little higher. "It's so good."

"It's bread."

"I assure you, my lord, there is nothing like the taste of a fine loaf of warm bread. Indeed, I have rarely tasted anything so wonderful, and I believe I can feel the warmth down to my toes." Saying so, she glanced down, to find the eyes of his hound staring up at her.

She pulled the bread away from him and shifted her chair away, too.

"He will not take it," Lord Kirkheathe said. "Unless you drop it."

"Oh."

"You tremble?"

"My lord, I do not care for dogs, especially ones as big as that. The Reverend Mother had a large dog and he…" Her words trailed off as her husband continued to stare at her.

"Cadmus," he said as he turned back to his food.

"I beg your pardon, my lord?"

"My dog's name is Cadmus."

"Oh." She shifted her chair farther away from the beast, for she was not so willing to believe he would not grab her bread if she gave him half a chance, perhaps biting her in the process.

Another group of servants entered, all men, and all carrying jugs of what must be the wine. Still chewing on her bread, she watched as one of them filled her *mazer*.

Her uncle, she noted, immediately gulped his down.

Putting the wide mouth of the shallow vessel to her lips, she sipped.

The wine was even better than the bread, and as it moved down her throat, her whole body seemed to relax with the goodness of it.

She had never had such wonderful wine. Would everything served in Donhallow be as excellent tonight? And every day?

No, no, she thought as she drank more of the wine, tonight was special. A feast. Her wedding feast. With the husband she had not met until today, so grim and resolute beside her. Why, his dog was paying more attention to her than he.

Maybe she should have married the dog.

The *mazer* tipped as she giggled. She quickly tried to right it before she spilled wine on the beautiful white linen or her lovely gown. She might have succeeded, but a lean, familiar hand grabbed hold of it and took it away.

Lord Kirkheathe set it upon the table.

"Forgive me, my lord," she whispered. "I haven't had good wine in a very long time, either."

He didn't even glance at her. Wasn't he a grim fellow—and on their wedding night, too! To be sure, she wasn't Genevieve, but did he have to be so very serious?

"I apologize for kissing you, too," she went on. "I didn't think you would mind so much, or I wouldn't have done it. I won't do it again."

Slowly—very slowly—he turned toward her and slowly raised his left brow.

For all the wine she had sipped, her mouth suddenly went dry. And just as suddenly, she regretted saying she wouldn't kiss him again.

He deliberately pushed her *mazer* out of her reach with his long, strong fingers.

She swallowed hard and looked away. This was her wedding day, and soon it would be the wedding night. How her heart pounded! She could hear it in her ears and feel the heat of her blood racing through her body.

Desperate in a new way, she reached out and took hold of the *mazer,* downing the last of the wine in a gulp. "I'm very thirsty, my lord," she explained with quiet defiance, although she didn't dare to look him in the eye. "And warm."

"Are you?" he said, his harsh rasp of a voice a whisper.

"A little dizzy, too."

"Then eat more."

She nodded, and was thankful to see the servants bringing the main dishes. When the butler brought more wine, Lord Kirkheathe didn't stop him from filling her *mazer* again, as she thought he might.

"You set a very fine table, my lord," she offered as she enjoyed a venison pasty filled with meat and gravy. "Do you always eat so well, or is it because it is a feast?"

"Yes," he replied, his gaze surveying the hall with a scrutiny the servants seemed both to expect and fear, for they kept glancing at him, and then acting very busy whenever he looked in their direction.

"You always eat so well? I am amazed neither you nor your men are plump, then."

"It is a special feast."

"Oh."

He turned toward her.

"I'm sorry if I sounded disappointed," she said hastily. "I'm sure you have a most excellent cook and kitchen servants. Indeed, my lord, I could live upon that bread alone."

The corner of one lip jerked upward. "And the wine."

She flushed. "I'm not a sot, I assure you, my lord. The wine at the convent was always sour and flat. We could barely drink it. But this, this is so good."

She took another drink. Yes, indeed it was.

"It should be."

"It was expensive?"

He inclined his head in assent.

"Oh." Her uncle had led her to believe Lord Kirkheathe was rich. If he begrudged her drinking it, perhaps he was a miser, too. Maybe that was what her uncle had been about to tell her. That would also explain why there was no music, or minstrel, or troubadour telling tales for their entertainment.

She pushed the *mazer* away.

"Eat," he commanded, eyeing the food still left in her trencher.

"I would like to, but my stomach may burst," she said with genuine regret. "It is not used to such varied and rich fare, and I would not like to have indigestion tonight."

His brows lifted as if she had said a scandalous thing, and she blushed as the image of him taking her in his arms burst into her head.

She rose unsteadily. "I believe, my lord, if there is no entertainment, I shall retire."

"The evening is young."

"It has been a long and tiring day. Please stay with your men. Rual can help me."

His brow lowered a fraction and the hall grew quiet, except for her uncle, snoring, with his head on the table.

She didn't know what more to say or do; all she wanted was to be alone a little, away from his piercing eyes and the visions he inspired, to gather her thoughts and prepare for...what was to come.

She turned and the room seemed to shift. She grabbed the back of the chair to steady herself—and just as before, she felt his arms about her.

Only this time, he swept her right off her feet and into his arms.

"My lord!"

He said nothing, and his face betrayed nothing as he marched toward the tower steps. Shocked and giddy, she looked over his shoulder. His dog was right behind.

"Good night!" she called out, feeling a need to make some sort of farewell.

Lord Kirkheathe said not a word.

What must they be thinking in the hall? If he thought her kiss and her drinking undignified, what was this?

Enthusiasm?

Emboldened by that hope, she wound her arms about his neck as he carried her up the stairs. "When I was a little girl," she confessed, "I used to dream of being swept off my feet. I didn't think it would really happen, though, and if you had described this to me a fortnight ago, I would have said you were mad."

Her husband didn't reply.

"I think we both forgot our manners today."

Still no response. He just marched stoically upward.

"You could have let me go with Rual."

"You might have fallen."

"I'm not drunk," she protested.

"No?"

"Absolutely not. I told you, it was the rich food." She leaned her head against his broad chest, the wool slightly rough against her cheek. "And perhaps the wine—a little. Don't be angry with me, please, my lord. I promise I will do better tomorrow. It has been a very strange day.''

Was he laughing?

She drew back and studied him. No, she must have been mistaken.

They reached the bedchamber and he pushed open the door with his foot, then waited as Cadmus trotted into the room.

''Does he sleep here, too?''

Her husband nodded. ''Guards the door.''

''Can he not do that from outside?''

''He looks for intruders.''

Elizabeth struggled out of his arms. ''You have intruders?''

''I am cautious,'' he said. He steadied her as her feet touched the ground.

''Oh.'' The tower seemed very cold when she was not in his arms.

Cadmus appeared at the door, panting.

''I suppose that means it is safe?''

''Yes.''

''Well, that is a relief, I must say. Although I think a man would have to be mad to try to attack you in your own castle.''

''A man might be,'' he agreed as he walked into the room ahead of her.

She followed him, noting that now a candleholder bearing several beeswax candles illuminated the room. The sight of his back and the realization he was undoing his wide leather belt made her hesitate on the threshold.

He glanced back at her over his shoulder. "He won't bite."

"I hope not."

His lips twitched. "I will not, either."

She smiled, albeit warily, as she sidled farther into the room. To avoid the big dog on her right, she would have to go toward the bed. Or toward her husband, who was even now tossing his belt on the chest near the narrow window. What a choice!

She shouldn't have insisted on getting married today. Tomorrow would have done just as well, and given her more time to get used to the idea....

What in the name of the saints was wrong with her? she thought, suddenly annoyed with herself. One more day wouldn't have made a difference in her feelings, and another day might have seen her sent back to the convent.

God's rood, this marriage was the best thing that had happened to her. What kind of silly little fool was she becoming, to be so coy and shy? Even if this man was a stranger to her, he was a very thrilling stranger.

With new determination, she briskly untied the lacing at the sides of the beautiful gown and drew it off. She boldly marched past her husband, and with care, laid the garment on the chest beside his belt. Then, clad in her thin shift, she climbed into the bed.

And watched the groom disrobe.

Chapter Five

Elizabeth Perronet was undoubtedly the strangest woman he had ever met, Raymond decided as he purposefully ignored her. It was as if she had no idea of what she was doing, or how her actions might be interpreted by those around her.

More importantly, it was as if she had no concept of dignity and the respect due to him, her lord and her husband.

Kissing him like that, for one thing, he silently grumbled as he tugged off his long tunic and threw it over the chest on top of the velvet gown and his leather belt. He didn't want her to kiss him, not then and not ever. Tonight he would take her as swiftly as he could, and with as little intimacy as possible.

She didn't want people to think she had been forced to marry him? What in the name of God did it matter what his people thought? He was their lord, their governor and protector. That was all they needed to know and remember.

Then to get nearly drunk! By God, she had just about fallen in the hall. There was no excuse for that. He had to pick her up and carry her away before she disgraced him entirely.

Half-naked, he washed his face with the cold water in the basin.

His body had, of course, reacted to the sensation of her body in his arms. It would to any woman in a similar situation. And when she leaned her head against him as if she felt safe with him—

He didn't want her to feel safe with him, just as he would never feel safe with her, lest she betray him, too.

God save him, how could he forget that harsh lesson, even when she spoke so winningly as he held her, her casual observation that it had been a "strange day" actually making him chuckle?

Then take her and be done, his mind commanded. Consummate the marriage as if it were any other bargain. Why hesitate? Why not simply go to bed?

He whirled around—to find Elizabeth unabashedly staring at him as she sat in his bed, his covers pulled up over her breasts, her long, waving hair flowing about her, her bright eyes gleaming. "You've got a lot of scars," she observed.

Suddenly, he felt more than half-naked, which was utterly ridiculous. He was no youth with his first woman!

He strode to the bed, sat on it and yanked off his boots.

He jumped when she ran a finger along one of the scars on his back. "Don't!" he snarled.

He heard the ropes creak as she moved back.

He rose and removed his breeches, dropping them on the floor. He turned around, facing her.

"I've never seen a naked man before," she whispered, staring at him. "Are they all like you?"

Without answering, he lifted the sheets and got in. He moved on top of her and shoved her shift out of the way.

Then he closed his eyes and imagined the first woman he had been with, an accommodating serving wench. He had been fourteen. Gildred had been very accommodating.

He remembered that day with Gildred in the orchard, when he had learned a mouth could do more than eat and drink and speak and kiss.

His bride was moist, but there was a barrier. So, she was indeed a virgin. Good.

He slowed a moment, then pushed. He heard a gasp, but no other cry. He started to thrust, slowly at first, then faster, and Elizabeth began to move in rhythm with him.

Gildred's mouth.

Elizabeth's parted lips. Her panting breath hot on him.

Gildred's lips upon him.

Elizabeth beneath him, her legs wrapped around him, eagerly pulling him closer. Her soft moans. Her hands clutching him. Her low groan of desire.

Not Gildred. Elizabeth.

Elizabeth…Elizabeth…Elizabeth.

With a low growl, he climaxed.

Panting, he opened his eyes, to find his wife's wide-eyed gaze upon his face.

Suddenly, as he looked down into her eyes, his manhood still within her, he wanted to press his lips against hers, to kiss her passionately and hold her close.

"Is that all?" she whispered.

Raymond abruptly withdrew and rolled off her, to the farthest edge of the bed, his back to her. "Yes."

"I hope we made a child," she said with a happy sigh as she pushed down her shift.

God's wounds, she was so ignorant she didn't realize he had taken her with all the finesse of a drunken soldier with a cheap whore.

"Sleep well, my lord," she murmured as she turned on her side.

He didn't answer.

Nor did he sleep well.

Elizabeth opened her eyes to find a hound of hell panting in her face.

She tried to scream, but no sound would come.

"Cadmus!" her husband barked.

She should have realized she was not having another nightmare back in the convent, because she was warm and well covered. And sore. Feeling foolish, she gingerly sat up.

Lord Kirkheathe, dressed in that same long, black tunic, regarded her from near the door, his dog at his side.

Was it possible for a dog to smirk?

At least her husband wasn't. "Don't be afraid of him."

She pulled the heavy coverings up under her chin, enjoying the comfort of their warmth. "I'll try not to be, but I was bitten very badly once," she explained.

He was going to see the scar sooner or later, she thought with resignation, so she untied the drawstring at the neck of her shift and eased it off her left shoulder, revealing the ugly red and puckered mark made by the Reverend Mother's pampered brute of a dog.

His eyes narrowed as he approached the bed. "A dog did that?"

She nodded.

He leaned even closer, examining her naked skin. Embarrassed by his scrutiny and mindful of what else he might see, she quickly pulled her shift back into place.

"Those other scars?"

She supposed he would have seen them sooner or later, too. Nevertheless, she couldn't meet his steadfast gaze. "I stole things at the convent and was duly punished."

"You, a thief?"

She shrugged. "We were always hungry and the little girls would weep so..."

"You stole food?" He sat beside her on the bed.

She raised her eyes, but could not tell if he approved, or was disgusted by her dishonesty. It was a very grave sin to steal from holy women, although in her heart she did not regret it for a moment. "All I could get, whenever I could get it," she admitted.

"For others?"

It was very tempting to tell him she never touched a morsel, but she could believe this man, with his intense and penetrating gaze, would know if she lied. "I ate of it."

He picked up her hand. His calluses felt rough against her skin as he examined her thin arms. "Not much."

"Enough," she whispered, half-afraid to speak in case it made him stop holding her.

His gaze met hers. "Cadmus will sleep on the other side of the door."

She couldn't help the sigh of relief that escaped her lips. "Thank you. I shall try to get used to him, my lord, so that he doesn't have to be exiled forever."

He smiled a little and heat trembled along her limbs.

Then noises from the courtyard caught his attention. He dropped her hand and went to the window to look outside.

Feeling bereft and thinking it must be getting near

time for mass, she threw back the covers, then shivered as the cool air hit her body.

"Stay," her husband ordered as he faced her, in much the same way he commanded his dog.

"My lord?" she asked warily.

"Stay in bed."

"It is so late in the day already," she replied. She gasped as her bare feet touched the stone floor and wrapped her arms about herself as she continued. "Surely there are things I should be doing. The servants will think I am lazy. That would a terrible way to begin."

"No one will disturb you."

"I beg your pardon?"

"Stay in bed as long as you like today. Call for Rual when you are ready."

She couldn't say what shocked her more: the notion that she could climb back into that warm, soft cocoon of a bed, or that he had said so much at once. "But mass—"

"Is over."

"For certain?"

He nodded.

"You do not fear the servants will think me slovenly?"

He shook his head.

Of course, she thought, he would not fear the servants.

And neither, Lady Katherine would say, should

she. So why not take advantage of his offer and indulge herself?

She scrambled back into the bed and, snuggling down into the featherbed, gave him a delighted smile. "Thank you, my lord. I cannot say how many times I imagined such a luxury as this."

"You will sleep?"

"Sleep? Oh, no, for then I would not know what I was enjoying."

His lips jerked into another little smile. "As you wish."

She sighed rapturously. "First the beautiful gown and now this! My lord, I thank you from the bottom of my heart, and I bless you for marrying me."

Lord Kirkheathe didn't answer as he strode from the room.

Sighing again, Elizabeth pulled the covers even tighter and contemplated her unusual husband. Seeing him smile, though it be a little one, made her want to laugh.

No doubt he had many cares, being such a rich and powerful lord. She would do what she could to lessen them, especially if she could see him smile more often.

Maybe a child would make him happier, too.

She climbed out of the bed, noting the dried blood on the sheet as she knelt.

"Dear God," she prayed, wishing she had gone to mass, the better for her prayer, and also that she had been a more humble, obedient person and thus more deserving, "let me be with child. If not already, soon!"

Fearing she had sounded too demanding, she added, "If it be Your will."

Shivering, she got up. Outside, the sound of horses and jingling harness took her to the window.

Her husband sat upon a mighty stallion. Behind him was a troop of mounted soldiers. She watched as Lord Kirkheathe raised his hand and moved toward the massive gates, his well-equipped men following.

He had not called out an order, merely raised his gloved hand and gestured. All was done with purposeful silence—and the instant obedience of well-trained and disciplined men.

With a grin, she realized the Reverend Mother would surely approve of her husband, and just as surely think he had made a poor choice of bride.

But the Reverend Mother was far away, and she was married, and soon—please, God, soon!—she might be a mother, looking after her children with love and kindness, as her parents had raised her before their deaths from fever when she was but eight years old.

Sighing, she blocked out the memories that came after that, of traveling from relative to relative, never really wanted or cared for. Of the brief respite at Lady Katherine's, who was strict, but fair.

Then the horrid years at the convent.

She turned and looked at the inviting bed, but

there was no point now to go back. Nor did she wish to give the servants any cause to disparage her, despite her husband's remarks on that point. She might as well dress and go to the hall.

Besides, if breakfast was half so good as the feast...

She slipped her feet into her shoes beside the bed and ran eagerly to the door. "Rual!"

The woman appeared so quickly, Elizabeth thought she must have been waiting on the stairs for her summons. "My lady?"

"I was to call for you when I was ready," she said jovially. "Well, I am ready. Do you know where my other dress has gone? I cannot wear the velvet gown today."

"Your old dress is in the chest beside the bed," Rual said as she came into the room.

"And all my other goods?"

"There, too."

"They don't take up much room, do they?" Elizabeth noted as she opened the chest.

"Shall I fetch warm water, my lady?"

"Do not trouble yourself. I am used to cold." No lie, that, Elizabeth thought ruefully as she put on her warm stockings and then her gray woolen gown. With the speed of years of familiarity, she tied the laces while Rual began to gather up the bedding.

Thinking of the dried blood, Elizabeth hurried to wash her face and hide her silly blush. After all,

Rual was a grown woman. She would know what had happened.

Everybody would know.

She splashed the water over her face, again and again, until she felt the heat diminish.

She picked up the small square of linen beside the basin and wiped off her face.

It smelled of him, her husband, Lord Kirkheathe....

"By our Lady," she muttered. *I don't even know his first name.*

"Do you need anything else, my lady?" Rual asked, holding the big bundle of cloth against her broad hip.

"No...well, yes," she confessed as she went to the chest and found her scarf and wimple. She didn't want to appear ignorant, but wouldn't it be worse not to know? "I fear in all the hurry yesterday, I didn't ask my husband's Christian name," she said as she put the scarf over her head and attached the wimple beneath her chin.

"Raymond D'Estienne is his Christian name, my lady, like his father before him."

"Did you know his parents?"

"No. They both died well before my time here."

"What do they say about them?"

The maidservant shrugged. "His father was reckoned a good man, although basely born."

"How did he come to have such an estate then?"

"It was taken from another and given to him by the earl of Chesney."

"You do not think he deserved it?"

"That is not for me to say, my lady. The earl thought he did."

"And his mother?"

"She died giving birth to him. His father did not marry again, like he did."

Elizabeth tried not to look shocked, but she suddenly felt off balance and unsteady, as if she were trying to cross a raging river on a fallen tree trunk.

Yet why should she be so surprised, she reasoned. He was not a young man. Of course he might have been married before, perhaps more than once. "How many wives has he had?"

"Just the one, other than you."

That was something at least. "Did she die in childbirth, too?"

"No, my lady."

"Was it an illness?"

"No, my lady. He killed her."

Chapter Six

Elizabeth didn't want to believe she had heard aright. "What did you say?"

"He killed her, in this very room."

Elizabeth went to stand face-to-face with Rual. "Why?"

"He said she tried to kill him, my lady." Rual shifted the bundle to the other hip. "The tale I heard, he claimed she drugged his wine and when he slept, she put a leather strap around his throat and tried to strangle him. He pushed her off and she fell and struck her head and died."

"That is why he has that scar around his neck," she murmured, "and sounds as he does." Her eyes narrowed as she regarded Rual. "You don't believe his explanation?"

"He has a temper."

"Was he brought before the king's justice for murder?"

"No."

"So what he said must be considered the truth."

"He is a lord."

"There is still punishment for a lord who kills his wife," she reminded Rual. "Had he struck her before?"

"There were no marks on her, my lady—at least none that people ever saw."

Which did not mean they were not there, beneath the woman's gown, or that he was not cruel to her in other ways. "Was he harsh with her?"

"Not that I've heard, my lady."

Again, that only meant not in public. However, considering the open nature of a lord and lady's life, the servants would know if things were seriously amiss between them. "He has his scar and ruined voice for proof that he was attacked."

The woman flushed and remained silent.

"Why did she want to kill him?"

"I don't know," the woman mumbled.

"Rual, if you don't believe my husband's explanation, you must have some reason to think he wanted her dead."

"Perhaps he suspected her of infidelity."

"With whom?"

Rual shrugged.

"Does anybody hazard a guess?"

"No, my lady."

Elizabeth sighed with relief. If there had been infidelity, or more than the merest suspicion of it—or any other hint of a motive on Lord Kirkheathe's part for wanting his wife dead—rumor and gossip would have flown from one part of this castle to the other. She had learned that well enough.

Rual shifted nervously. ''My lady, I think I had best get these linens below.''

''Thank you, Rual,'' Elizabeth replied, seeing the wisdom of Lady Katherine's admonition never to listen to the gossip of servants, no matter how tempting. ''Has my uncle eaten this morning?''

''He and his men departed at first light on my lord's orders.''

Elizabeth stared at her incredulously. ''He is already gone?''

''Once Lord Kirkheathe got the dowry, he sent him off, with his men grumbling all the while. Your uncle felt so sleepy and poorly from the wine, he could barely keep his seat.''

''But Lord Kirkheathe was here when I awoke.''

''Came back, that's all.''

''I didn't hear a thing.''

Rual smirked. ''You were sleeping sound, I expect.''

''I suppose,'' Elizabeth replied, paying little heed to Rual's expression as she wondered how long he had been there, watching her.

''Have you no warmer gown, my lady?''

''No. The hall will have a fire, will it not?'' Elizabeth answered.

''Aye, a good one. Lord Kirkheathe insists upon it.''

"Then I shall go there and get warm," Elizabeth said. "And when you are done with the laundress, will you come back and show me about my new home?"

"Aye, my lady."

"There, my lord, do you see?" Aiken said, pointing at the footings of the bridge. "It's rotting. The bridge'll collapse come spring."

Holding his tunic up out of the mud of the riverbank with one hand, Raymond noted the decayed wood.

Thank God, he had the money to pay for repairs. Or, to be more precise, thank Elizabeth's uncle, who had no notion of just how desperately Raymond needed money, or he would have haggled the dowry lower. Now, however, Raymond could afford much-needed repairs to various buildings, roads and bridges on his estate.

Of course, he could have haggled the dowry higher, Raymond thought, had he not believed that if he did so, Perronet was enough of a miser to cancel the contract and take her back to the convent. She had been so adamant about not returning, he would have had to be made of iron to ignore her pleas.

If he had been made of iron, he could have ignored her this morning, and not stood watching her sleep like some sort of besotted simpleton.

Yet how sweet she had looked, her hair spread

upon the pillow, one arm thrown across his side of the bed as if she would embrace him if he were there.

He thought of the scar of the dog bite, and the long, narrow welts on her back.

God's blood, what kind of nun inflicted beatings to make scars like that?

The kind he would like to meet and show the error of her ways.

He straightened. "How many more are rotting?"

"Ten, I make it, my lord," Aiken said, scrambling up to higher ground. He was a short man of brisk movements, and although he was a soldier, he was also the finest judge of structures, whether wood or stone, Raymond had met in his life. "They'll all need replacing this summer. Best time is August, when the water's low. They should last some weeks yet, though."

"Good."

As Raymond climbed up the bank, he glanced up at the sky. Nearly noon. Time to go back home.

Home.

For the first time in fifteen years, it actually felt that way.

The hoofbeats on the road interrupted his reverie, and a band of mounted men appeared, Fane Montross at their head.

Drawing his sword, Raymond strode to the center of the road and waited for his neighbor, former friend and detested enemy to approach.

Montross signaled his men to halt. "Why, Raymond, this is unexpected," he called out from the back of his prancing stallion.

Raymond ran a scornful gaze over Montross. As always, he was extravagantly dressed, this time in Lincoln green and gold, for he was as vain as Allicia had been.

He was also as fair as she, with handsome features and curling blond hair.

"I would have expected the bridegroom to be at home today of all days," Montross noted with a mocking smile.

So, he had heard of his marriage. Not unexpected, but Raymond begrudged him the knowledge nonetheless.

"That is, of course, why I have set foot upon your land. I have come to wish you joy."

"With twenty soldiers?"

"A proper guard, that's all. We all know these are troubled times and men must take precautions. You have ten men yourself, and you are on your own land."

Raymond would not explain that they were masons and carpenters assessing the state of the bridges on his estate, any more than he would explain anything he did to Fane Montross.

"Surely you are going to be chivalrous and invite me to meet your bride?"

Raymond would rather tell Montross to go to the devil and take his twenty men with him. That, how-

ever, would be to make the first hostile move, and
he would never do that. "Please do," he said, turning toward his horse, Castor.

He glanced at Aiken. "You and four others, ride
behind Montross's men."

"As you wish, my lord," Aiken said as a significant look passed between them. "We wouldn't
want any of them to get lost, would we?"

Raymond smirked, then signaled his men to start
off toward home.

"Are there any more storerooms?" Elizabeth
asked Rual, who looked as weary as she.

"No, my lady."

Elizabeth tried not to smile at that, but in truth,
she was glad. She doubted she would be able to
remember half of all that Rual had shown her of
Donhallow, or remember the names of all the people
to whom she had been introduced. She would do her
best to remember the most important; others had
made more of a memorable impression.

There was Hale, the serjeant-at-arms and second
in command of the castle garrison. He was a broad-
shouldered, gruff fellow, yet he had smiled at her
kindly, in a way that warmed her heart.

The mews had been interesting, because there had
been no such place in the convent. Her husband
didn't have many birds, but the few he had were
fine ones, she thought. The fowler, a very small man
with very beady eyes, hadn't said much. He had

simply stood and watched them, just like his charges.

Meeting Lud, the cook, and the kitchen servants had been much more pleasant. Lud had been pleased by her sincere praise for his efforts, and the servants in the kitchen, while as disciplined as all in Donhallow, seemed to enjoy their duties.

The same could be said of most of the female servants, with the possible exception of Greta, who was in charge of the laundry. She was a thin, nervous woman whose head bobbed and eyes darted and fingers twitched. Elizabeth had been tempted to assure the woman that if things were not perfectly clean, that would not be cause for instant dismissal. Then she realized, based on the half smiles of the other laundresses, that Greta must be one of those people who would be taut as a bowstring no matter what she did. Moreover, it would not be wise to imply that the new chatelaine might be willing to overlook shoddy work of any kind.

Nevertheless, she had smiled and tried to put the woman at ease. Unfortunately, it seemed Greta's tension was catching, and Elizabeth was very relieved to finally leave the laundry.

Yes, the day had been a long one, and as they exited the dungeon where food was stored, Elizabeth was looking forward to sitting down to the noon meal.

She thought she might even be glad that she would not be called upon to speak much to her husband. Donhallow Castle was so vast and so populous, she was feeling distinctly overwhelmed.

As she walked beside Rual toward the great hall, she noticed a peddler's cart near the entrance. A man stood beside it, speaking to the guards. Sitting on a seat in the cart was a thin, pale woman holding a baby.

Elizabeth uttered a small cry of delight and hurried toward them. The men fell silent as she approached, and the woman watched her warily. The baby started to bawl, perhaps because the mother's hold had grown too tight.

Elizabeth smiled at her to put her at her ease, even as she noted that the young mother looked as if she had not had rest or a good meal in days. "Please, may I hold him? Or is it a girl?"

"It's a boy, my lady," the woman shyly replied.

"She's Lady Kirkheathe," one of the guards muttered to the woman. "Do as she—"

Elizabeth silenced him with a glance. "I adore babies," she explained. "If you would rather continue to hold him yourself, I understand."

"My lady!" Rual panted as she arrived. "Lord Kirkheathe does not encourage peddlers."

The man beside the guards gave her a sour look. His matted hair and patched clothes did not improve the impression he was making, and his wagon contained what looked to be bits and baubles, cheap and flimsy and useless. However, it was not the peddler or his wares that mattered to Elizabeth.

"I didn't say I wanted to buy anything," Elizabeth said before turning back to the woman. "Please, may I hold him?"

"If ye're not going t'buy, we better not stay," the peddler grumbled.

Elizabeth and the woman glanced at him, then smiled at each other, and the woman carefully handed down her son.

Elizabeth moved the tattered blanket away from his little face. He was a well-made child, with a shock of dark hair and plump, pink cheeks. "Oh, he is lovely!"

The baby opened his eyes and started to cry even more loud and lustily. The woman nervously bit her lip.

"His crying doesn't bother me," Elizabeth assured her.

Patting the baby's back, she started to rock from side to side. She didn't know why she moved that way; it just felt right.

Suddenly, the infant stopped crying, gave a tremendous burp and settled against Elizabeth's shoulder. She smiled at the woman. "Wind, that's all."

The woman nodded while the peddler frowned.

"Since I have no money of my own, I cannot buy anything, but there is no reason you cannot stay here for a night, and eat with the servants in the kitchen. My husband sets a very fine table. Please say you'll stay and let me hold little...?"

"Erick," the woman said softly.

"Little Erick some more?"

The woman looked anxiously at her husband. "Well, a free meal is a free meal," he muttered with a shrug of his thin shoulders.

"My lady," Rual said pointedly, and as if the peddler and his wife were deaf, "I don't think Lord Kirkheathe will agree with that. He'll think you're encouraging them."

The servant's warning gave her pause. However, another look at Erick's thin and tired mother told her what she had to do. "Let me worry about my husband's approval, Rual. For now, they may stay."

"You'll find out what he thinks soon enough," Rual grumbled as she nodded at the gate.

They all watched as Lord Kirkheathe and his men rode into the courtyard.

How imposing and imperial he looked mounted on a huge black horse, like a king or emperor.

There was another man, also mounted on a fine horse, just behind him. The stranger was flamboyantly dressed in a short tunic of bright green and gold, with a velvet cloak thrown back over his shoulder.

In among her husband's men were others she did not recognize from the hall. They must belong to the stranger, who was scrutinizing the castle and trying to look as if he wasn't.

Not a friend.

And there was more to his scrutiny than mere study.

Envy. Oh, yes, envy. She had seen that look a thousand times at the convent among the girls who competed for the Reverend Mother's favor and what gifts she had to bestow.

Elizabeth had been spared that feeling because she knew she could never hope to win favor, but she had watched the others, and knew what she was seeing.

The look her husband shot the stranger as he dismounted confirmed that they were not friends.

As for the stranger, for all his smiles and chatter that she could not quite distinguish above the sound of the horse and harness, he was tense. Battle-ready, was the expression that came to Elizabeth's mind.

And then her husband saw her. A shiver of alarm ran down her back. Would he be angry that she had offered some small hospitality to the peddler and his family?

He did not look angry. In fact, she could read nothing at all in his expression.

Then his eyes narrowed slightly as he gestured for her to come to him. She wished she had not noticed Erick and his parents—but she had, and it was not wrong to offer them a bit of food.

Elizabeth handed Erick back to his mother. "Stay unless you are told otherwise," she said quietly, then turned and prepared to make the best of things.

As she approached, the stranger ran his gaze over her and on his face she saw…surprise.

Her hair must be a wild, curling mess. She had

taken off her scarf and wimple and tucked them in
her belt when she had been in the laundry, where
the air was hot and damp from the fires warming
the water. The steam also made her horrid old gray
gown damp, and she had sneezed so much, her nose
must be as red as the stranger's boots.

If the stranger were a friend, it might not matter—
but he wasn't. Lord Kirkheathe was a proud man,
and surely he would not be pleased to have his ugly
wife looking disheveled and more like a servant than
some of the servants.

That thought rankled like an arrow's tip in her
breast and she flushed with shame. Not for herself—
she had long known she was unattractive and unfortunately, there was nothing she could do about
her appearance.

"Elizabeth, this man is Sir Fane Montross," her
husband said as she reached them. "Montross, my
wife, Elizabeth."

She bowed. "I am honored, sir."

"It is I who am honored, my lady," the blond
man said with an even greater bow and what she
thought was a snide little smile. "I could not rest
until I had seen Raymond's young and beautiful
bride."

"Are you married, sir?"

Her question startled him, and she was glad. "No,
my lady, I regret that I have not been so fortunate."

"I see," she said in a tone that implied she could

understand why—and the reason was not a flattering one.

Then she slipped her hand into her husband's, praying all the while he would remain his inscrutable self and not shy away. "You will stay and dine with us, of course?"

She felt her husband stiffen. Had she gone too far?

"Dine? Why, I shall be delighted. It has been many years since I have had the pleasure of supping in Donhallow Castle."

"No doubt because men can become quite boorish if they're without female companionship for a long time," she noted, running her other hand up her husband's muscular arm and looking into his face adoringly. She might not be pretty, but she could give this impertinent, vain fellow a reason to think her husband need not be pitied.

Her husband's dark eyes regarded her with a hint of...interest? Perhaps even amusement?

"Oh, I think you need not fear that in his case, my lady," Montross replied. "He has never lacked for female companionship."

If she had loved her husband, that would have been a very hurtful thing to say. As it was, it did hurt, just not so much as it might have. After all, she had assured her husband-to-be that he could take a mistress after they were wed, and she would not mind. She could not, therefore, protest what he had done before they were married.

She turned to Montross with a patronizing smile that would have done credit to the Reverend Mother herself. "For a man as virile as my husband, one could expect nothing else."

"Kirkheathe is fortunate to have so forgiving a bride."

"It is I who am fortunate," she replied. "Very happy and very blessed," she cooed, giving her husband another look of adoration.

"I had heard, my lady, that you come from a convent."

"I did," she said, caressing her husband's forearm, "and if I had known what I was missing, I would have run away years ago." She gave Montross a bold, triumphant smile. "But then I would not be married to my lord, so I think it is better I stayed in the convent until my uncle came to bring me here. Do you not agree?"

Chapter Seven

Standing in his courtyard with his bride caressing him in front of everybody, utterly confounding Montross—and him, too, truth be told—Raymond wondered how long he should let this bizarre conversation continue.

Surprisingly, however, he was enjoying this strange situation. He was especially delighted and amused by the consternation on Fane Montross's face. He had always been full of himself and possessed a snide tongue, yet who would have guessed Elizabeth, who had been locked away from the world for so long, would prove a match for his worldly and sophisticated enemy?

And who would have guessed that he would not find a public display of affection an embarrassment, but actually arousing?

"I did not hear you were so happy," Montross remarked.

Elizabeth laughed again. "It would seem gossip

flies as swift as a hawk about these parts if you have heard so soon about the state of our marriage. Surely you do not give much credit to gossip, sir. I can assure you, after all my years in the convent, that I do not.''

"I have heard it said there is usually a grain of truth in it,'' Montross retorted, as nonplussed as Raymond had ever seen him.

"Well, I suppose there may be in some cases, but they are very rare. Besides, my husband can have no doubts of my happiness about our marriage after last night, can you, my lord?''

She smiled as she lowered her eyelids, looking for all the world as if she were both embarrassed and delighted. The implication was unmistakable: that their wedding night had been bliss.

She was astonishing. Absolutely astonishing! Who could guess what she might say next?

Then she tilted her head and gave him a questioning glance.

God's wounds, she wanted him to answer, Raymond thought with a jolt of dismay.

He would not announce his feelings for everyone to hear.

Yet as she continued to regard him with her brilliant eyes, and as Montross shifted impatiently, he was suddenly overcome by a need to respond in some fashion. So, lifting Elizabeth's hand to his lips, Raymond softly kissed it.

He let his lips linger, wanting to keep them there

for a long time. Then slide his mouth toward her warm palm, continuing slowly, slowly toward her slender wrist…

Elizabeth blushed. From so simple a thing as a kiss on the hand? What would she do if he—?

Startled at the tremendous rush of heated desire firing his loins, he straightened.

"Oh, you must forgive me, sir," Elizabeth said, her face still flushed as she turned toward Montross. "We should not be standing in the courtyard. Please, come with us to our hall."

Our hall, Raymond thought as they led the way, Montross trailing behind.

Their hall. If ever a woman seemed worthy to share his estate, his home and his bed…

Had he not thought that of Allicia, too?

As they entered the hall, Elizabeth paused and whispered, "Forgive me, my lord, for looking as I do."

He supposed she must mean that hideous dress she wore, although he had only noticed it now. It hung like a sack, belted with a cheap leather girdle that was knotted at the side. Tucked into the belt were squares of cloth. Her scarf, perhaps? If so, he was glad she was not wearing it. Her glorious hair waved about her face like she were a wild creature, untamed and free. It seemed a crime to cover it.

Montross came up behind them.

"If you will excuse me," Elizabeth said, addressing them both, "I will get out of this working gown and into something more suitable for receiving guests.''

With that, she briskly hurried away.

Without a word to Montross, Raymond headed for the dais, letting Montross follow him. When they reached the dais and Raymond gestured at the chair opposite him, the strangeness of the situation reasserted itself. He had vowed once that he would die before he would let Montross cross his threshold again, yet now he was here—and at the behest of his wife.

His beautiful, surprising wife.

Raymond sat in the chair that had been his father's, and Cadmus settled at his feet. They sat some moments in silence, until Montross spoke.

''Nothing seems to have changed. Same furnishings, same tapestries.''

Raymond didn't reply.

Montross fixed him with a pointed look. ''Tell me, does she know about Allicia?''

''That is between my wife and I.''

Montross's lips curved up into a sinister smile and he leaned closer, reminding Raymond of a snake poised to strike. ''She doesn't, does she?''

Raymond smiled.

Montross obviously didn't believe his unspoken denial, for he sat back, a smug grin of satisfaction on his face. ''Well, well, well. Perhaps she won't be quite so happy and loving when she learns what you did to my sister.''

"You are forgetting what Allicia nearly did to me," Raymond growled.

"Whatever the exact circumstances, she must have been miserable in her marriage to try to kill her husband. Perhaps that alone will give your wife pause."

His hands curling into fists, Raymond got to his feet. Cadmus rose just as swiftly, a growl rumbling in his throat.

"Oh, my lord, I am so sorry!" Elizabeth cried behind him.

He whirled around.

Dressed in the blue gown, her hair braided, Elizabeth hurried up to them. "I have ordered wine to be brought at once. I should have done so before I went to change my gown. Please forgive me for being so remiss." She glanced at Montross, who made a halfhearted attempt to rise before sitting again. "And I apologize to you, too, of course, sir," she murmured before returning her anxious gaze to her husband.

Raymond didn't know what to do. She thought he was angry she had not ordered wine? His wrath had absolutely nothing to do with her.

Except that he didn't want her to hear about Allicia from Fane Montross.

"I have told Rual to inform the kitchen servants about our guests, and to prepare extra places for them to sleep in the hall."

"We will not stay overnight," Montross muttered.

Raymond silently agreed. The king would abdicate before that happened. It was one thing to have the man here now, quite another to extend that hospitality any further.

On the other hand, he had sworn that Montross would not cross his threshold again, either. Maybe it was not a wise thing to make vows until he knew his wife better.

"No? Perhaps another time," Elizabeth replied with rather too much haste, and yet a pleasant enough smile that he could not be sure whether she was glad or not of Montross's refusal to her invitation.

"Nor, I think, shall we avail ourselves of your hospitality any longer," Montross continued, getting to his feet.

"I hope you do not find my welcome lacking?"

"Not yours, my lady. Truly, you are most kind," he said with another bow. "But your husband knows I will not sup with you, or sleep beneath your roof, because he killed my sister."

Raymond's hand went to his sword as he glanced at Elizabeth. A strange expression flitted across her face, and then it softened to one full of sympathy. "I understand, sir. The shame of having a sister who would do murder must be too great."

Raymond felt as if the dais had collapsed, while

Montross stared at her with unabashed shock, his mouth open and his eyes wide.

How had she heard about Allicia? From her uncle? How much did he know? What exactly had he told her?

Elizabeth went to Montross and patted him on the arm as she might a distraught child. "It must be very upsetting to have so wicked a sister. However, surely it is obvious that my husband is willing to overlook the past."

Now that the initial shock had subsided, Raymond felt the most outrageous urge to crow at the stunned disbelief on Montross's face. For years he had complained to all and sundry—and their overlord, the earl of Chesney, most of all—that Raymond was a cold-blooded killer who had murdered Allicia without good cause. He might have had more people believe him if not for the testimony of all in Donhallow, Raymond's honorable reputation and the evidence of Allicia's own crime in the scar around Raymond's throat, as well as his ruined voice.

Yet this was the first time Raymond had witnessed anybody telling Montross that he should be ashamed of his sister. He could kiss Elizabeth for that.

Enraged, his enemy looked from Elizabeth to him, then turned on his heel, called for his men, and marched out of the hall.

"My lord, I hope I didn't offend him too much,

or you,'' she said, looking up at Raymond doubtfully, all her bold spirit apparently gone.

If she thought him angry with her, she could not be more wrong. He took hold of her hand. ''Come.''

''Where are we—?''

''My solar.''

She didn't say anything more as he led her where only yesterday—although it seemed days ago—he had announced he would marry her.

Once inside the room, he shoved the door closed behind them.

She looked at him, her mien serious. ''I'm sorry if I embarrass you, my lord.''

She seemed skittish and more afraid than she had been before, and that troubled him greatly. ''How much do you know about Allicia?''

''I had a little talk with Rual this morning,'' Elizabeth confessed. ''Not a talk, exactly,'' she continued after a wary glance at his face. ''I asked her to tell me. She wasn't very eager, I assure you, my lord.'' She took another breath. ''At any rate, I asked her to tell me what she knew and she told me that you accidentally killed your wife after she drugged your wine and tried to strangle you.''

He nodded, once.

''I didn't know that man was her brother until he spoke in the hall. I realized you were enemies, of course, but I didn't understand why until then.'' Her eyes widened. ''You are not surprised that I guessed that, surely? It was very obvious, my lord, from the way you both acted. He hates and envies you, and you loathe him. Given that you killed his sister, albeit in self-defense, the hate is easy to understand." She slid him a shy look. "I confess I had some doubts about your claim of self-defense, for you are a warrior and your wife was but a woman."

"*Had* some doubts?"

"Her own brother dispelled them, for it is very clear to me that he would not hesitate to have you brought before the king's court if there had been a shred of evidence to accuse you of murder. Since that did not happen, I believe that you did not mean to kill her."

Raymond sighed, feeling a burden slip from his shoulders. "No, I did not."

She smiled a moment, then frowned. "Yet I also think his hate springs from the way he envies you, and I would guess he has envied you for a very long time."

How did she guess all that? "Are you a seer?"

"No. I could tell from the way he looked at Donhallow, and you."

And you, Raymond added inwardly, suddenly remembering Montross's eyes as he had stared at Elizabeth. At the time, he had been too perplexed, and then pleased, to really take note.

God knew they had wenched together enough in their youth that he should have remembered the expression in Montross's eyes when he found a woman pleasing.

Would Elizabeth betray him, too? She could. What man who saw her would not desire her?

What if another man took her from him?

A shaft of pure terror struck his heart.

She could hurt him, deeply.

No woman must ever hurt him again. He would be strong, not weak.

"I do not want you to be angry with me, my lord."

"Then do not give me cause."

"I shall try not to," she said in a small voice.

A vulnerable voice. The voice of a woman who wanted to please him, and instead had been rebuffed.

Her disappointment and dismay could not be helped, he told himself. He could lust after her and love her often, but fall in love and lose his heart to her he dare not.

He took her by the shoulders. She looked up at him questioningly, her bright eyes shining, just before his mouth swooped down upon hers in a passionate, heated kiss.

Despite his resolution, Elizabeth summoned up such desire and need and yearning....

Sweet heaven, he had not kissed a woman like this in years and years. Had not wanted to. Had not needed to.

She responded with equal fervor. Parting her lips, she relaxed into his embrace while his tongue penetrated the moist warmth of her mouth.

He had been a fool not to kiss her last night, or

caress her curvaceous body. He should have used his hands and lips to make her ready for him.

Now his hands moved slowly over her, exploring her. As his arm wrapped tightly about her, he pressed his fingers between her legs and rubbed gently. She moaned softly, the sound arousing him even more.

Still kissing her, he slid his hands under her skirt and beneath her buttocks, then lifted her. Her skirt bunched around her waist, she wrapped her bare legs about him as he carried her to the table. Slowly he lowered her, so that she sat upon the top.

He broke the kiss only long enough to hike up his tunic and free himself. Panting, she watched hungrily, her eyes gleaming like a cat's in the dark.

Then he was between her knees. She clutched his shoulders and her eyes closed in ecstasy as he entered her. "Oh, my lord!" she whispered when he started to thrust faster. "Oh, yes, please…do…that…"

And then she groaned and the sudden throbbing of her soft, hot honor sent him over the brink, too.

He collapsed against her, his breathing hoarse and his body damp with sweat.

She laid her head against his shoulder. "I hope this means I am forgiven for my impertinence in the courtyard."

"Yes," he whispered.

The warm breath of her sigh caressed his cheek. "I am glad, my lord, although if this were your idea of a punishment, I confess I would want to be impertinent all the time.''

Trying not to smile, he drew back and straightened his clothes.

Elizabeth looked down and gingerly got off the table. ''My gown! It is so wrinkled! Oh, no! I've ruined it,'' she said as she began to press it with her hands, running them over her thighs in a way that was incredibly exciting.

''*I* ruined it.''

Relief dawned in her eyes. ''You are not angry about this, either?''

He shook his head. God's wounds, he would ruin a dress every hour if he could do it this way.

She stopped trying to press out the wrinkles with her hand and swallowed hard, then straightened her slender shoulders. ''I think I had better confess something else,'' she said, her whole body tense as if she expected him to curse her, or worse. ''A peddler and his wife and child are in the kitchen, eating. Rual said you do not approve of peddlers. I did not buy anything,'' she hastened to add.

''I am not the Church,'' he growled, ''to dispense charity.''

''The woman looked so thin and tired, I feared she would fall ill—''

''You let them bring sickness here?'' he demanded, another kind of dread knotting his stomach. He should have asked who those people were and what they were doing in the courtyard instead of paying heed only to Elizabeth.

"I think all she needs is a few good meals, and the baby is not sick, nor—"

"The baby you held?" The baby that had looked so natural in her arms.

"Yes, my lord, he is a fine, healthy—"

Raymond didn't wait to hear more. He marched from the solar and headed straight to the kitchen, ignoring the stares of the servants, as well as Elizabeth trotting to keep up with him.

His father had died of a sickness brought to Donhallow by a peddler, and he nearly. And now Elizabeth had let a peddler and sick wife into his castle. She had held their child.

He strode into the kitchen and his gaze swept the room, passing quickly over his servants and the food being prepared to settle on the man, woman and child huddled in the corner.

"Out!" he commanded, glaring at them, wishing he could bellow his rage. "Out of Donhallow."

The man jumped to his feet and pulled the woman's arm. She was thin, as Elizabeth had said. The child she held to her shoulder started to cry.

"My lord, please do not be angry with them," Elizabeth pleaded as they scurried out. "It is my fault. Rual warned me."

As the servants cowered, he turned to glower at her.

"They are here now, so a little mercy—"

"Who is overlord here?"

"You, my lord.

"Remember that."

She nodded. "And I will remember what I said if you would marry me," she said quietly, regarding him with all the steadfastness of a battle-hardened warrior. "You rule here, my lord, and I was wrong to disobey your will. I shall not make that mistake again."

In light of her resolute expression, he wished he had not reacted so passionately.

Yet he would not have peddlers and beggars bringing their sicknesses, as well as chicanery and tricks, into his castle. He glanced sharply at the cook. "The meal is ready?"

"Aye, my lord," Lud stammered.

"Serve it."

He marched past Elizabeth toward the hall. Servants hurried to the hall after him, and in a moment, she heard the familiar banging of the trestle tables being set up in the hall.

The cook and his helpers, with several glances both pitying and wary, went back to their work.

Elizabeth grabbed a small loaf of coarse brown bread and hurried from the kitchen. She continued across the courtyard, the soft soles of her shoes slapping briskly against the cobblestones.

How could things have gone so wrong so quickly? This morning she had been so happy and sure she had made a wise decision leaving the convent. But now, after learning about her husband and seeing his fierce temper...witnessing his lack of generosity...knowing there was nothing she could do or say to criticize him because she had assured him she would be subservient to him...what a desperate fool she had been!

She swiped at the tear running down her cheek and swallowed hard as she approached the imposing gate. She didn't want the guards, or anybody else, to see her crying.

Nor should she cry. After all, she had chosen this path. Now she must walk it, come what may.

Chapter Eight

Tapping his foot, Raymond waited. And waited. The others gathered in the hall also waited, as silent as he as they surreptitiously eyed one another, and their overlord.

Ask where his wife had gone, he would not. That would mean he cared, and if he cared about that, they might believe he cared about her feelings. And if he cared about her feelings, that would give her power over him.

Where the devil was she? She had eaten like a starving woman last night. It didn't seem likely that she would care to miss a meal.

On the other hand, she was used to deprivation. If he had angered her enough, missing a meal in a display of childish pique would probably not trouble her overmuch—but if she thought such behavior was going to make him regret what he had done, she was very wrong.

"Rual," he growled at last, glancing sharply at the maidservant standing close by.

The startled woman jumped. "My lord?"

"Serve the food."

"But your lady—"

"Now."

Rual nodded rapidly and disappeared into the corridor leading into the kitchen. In a few short moments, she and the other serving maids dutifully appeared with the bread and butter.

Perhaps Elizabeth would return before the noon meal was over. If so, he would banish her from the hall until it was concluded. If she could not trouble herself to be here for the beginning, she could miss it entirely.

However, Elizabeth did not arrive during that course, or the next. Or the one after that.

What in God's name was she playing at? Surely she couldn't have been so foolish as to wander away from the castle? She knew that he had enemies.

Fane Montross would do anything to hurt him, if he had half a chance.

Fane Montross had looked at her with lust in his blue eyes.

If Fane Montross found her alone and unprotected—

Raymond's chair scraped over the stone floor as he abruptly rose. Without a word to his men, he strode out of the hall toward the gatehouse, Cadmus loping dutifully behind.

The two guards swiftly straightened when they saw him marching toward them.

"Aye, my lord," the more senior answered briskly when he halted in front of them.

"My wife?"

"She went past here, my lord."

"When?"

"Some time ago, my lord."

"Where was she going?"

"She didn't say, my lord."

The other man's gaze flickered and Raymond transfixed him with a glare.

"I saw her go to the village, my lord," the young man stammered.

"Alone?"

"Aye, my lord, alone."

"She never leaves Donhallow unescorted again."

"Yes, my lord," the guards replied in unison.

The commander of the garrison appeared at the door of the barracks and hurried toward them. "Is something amiss, my lord?" Barden asked.

"My wife is never to leave Donhallow alone again."

Barden's brows rose.

"If I am not back with her by the time the sun is below the west wall, begin to organize search parties."

"Aye, my lord," Barden replied.

There was no need to explain to him what Raymond dreaded; Barden had been a foot soldier in

Donhallow when Raymond was at his father's knee, and knew well the enmity between his overlord and Montross.

He was also the one who had found Raymond choking on his own blood as he knelt, horror-stricken, beside Allicia's dead body. It had been Barden's testimony to the earl of Chesney, as well as the wound to Raymond's throat, that had insured that Raymond was not brought before the king's justice, charged with his wife's murder.

"You think we should wait?" Barden asked.

"Yes."

Raymond continued toward the village. It could be that she was safely there, and he was worried for nothing.

The first few villagers who saw him march past stared, for their overlord never simply walked into the town. He was always with a troop of men, and usually mounted.

What would they make of him traipsing after his wayward wife? Raymond thought with growing frustration. They would think him ridiculous.

Nevertheless, he continued his search, ignoring the shock and surprise on the villagers' faces. More than one who caught sight of his grim visage turned and fled as he approached.

Where in the name of God had Elizabeth gone? It was as if the earth had opened up and swallowed her.

Or somebody had taken her.

Maybe Barden was right, and he was wrong to wait. Wiping the perspiration from his forehead, Raymond was about to turn back when he heard her voice.

She was singing.

He knew the song, too. It was a ballad about ill-fated lovers. He had liked to sing it in his youth, especially when he had courted Allicia, in the days when his voice was fine and strong.

Who was Elizabeth singing to? Who was accompanying her honey-smooth voice on a harp, as he had played for Allicia?

He followed the music to the end of a deserted lane. She was in the last wattle and daub building near the village wall. The shutter was off the window closest to him, and the door past it stood open.

The music stopped and she laughed, the sound a lovely light trill.

Raymond cautiously peered around the side of the window into a barren workroom that housed pieces of wood and partially completed instruments. A man so old he looked as if he might have apprenticed for Noah sat at a workbench covered in tools, bits of wood and sawdust.

He didn't even know there was an instrument maker in the village.

Near the old man, on a low stool, sat Elizabeth, holding a harp made of pale blond wood. A shaft of sunlight came in through an upper window, encompassing her in its brilliance.

"You play well, my lady," the elderly man wheezed.

"You are too kind, Johannes. It is very obvious I have not played the harp in a long time. I could barely remember the words to the song."

"Your voice is like the angels', my lady."

She not only sang like an angel, Raymond thought. She looked like one.

What was he doing, acting like some kind of spy, creeping down lanes and peering through windows? This was his wife, in *his* village protected by *his* castle.

He marched into the room. With a gasp, Elizabeth jumped to her feet, dropping the harp, which hit the hard dirt floor.

Meanwhile, the old man, breathing hard, struggled to stand.

"This is my husband, Lord Kirkheathe," Elizabeth said after she had collected herself, and as if this old instrument maker were a noble of the court. "My lord, this is Johannes. He makes harps."

"Come," was all the response Raymond made as he reached out to take her by the arm.

She moved out of the way with an alacrity that would have done credit to a master swordsman. "Thank you for letting me play, Johannes," she said as she picked up the fallen instrument and put it in his hands. "I am glad the harp didn't break."

The man held out the instrument as if he meant

her to take it, but before she could, Raymond stepped between them, glowering at her. "Come."

He discovered his bride had quite a glower herself. However, she said not a word, just turned on her heel and went out the door.

He hurried after her and pulled her to a stop in the lane. "Don't ever leave Donhallow alone again," he growled.

She met his gaze boldly. "Am I a prisoner?"

He had never met such a defiant woman. "You know you are not."

"Then why am I to be treated like one?"

She must have utterly confounded the Reverend Mother at that convent, who was no doubt used to unfailing obedience, as he was.

He could sympathize with the woman's frustration, but even so, he suddenly realized, he admired Elizabeth's mettle more. "You need a guard."

"Even here?"

He nodded once.

"I did not think I would be in danger in our own village."

"*Did* you think?" he countered.

Her passionate gaze faltered at last. "Perhaps I thought my noble husband was so angry and upset with me, I would give him indigestion if I broke bread with him."

He gave her a skeptical look.

"Or perhaps not. Perhaps I thought, I do not care

to eat with him when he is in such a mood. Therefore, I will go to the village.''

"Without permission."

"Yes, my lord, without permission.''

He came closer to her, and as he did, the sight of a tendril of her hair on her soft, flushed cheek nearly made him forget what he was about to say, and why he had been so angry. "Remember I have enemies, Elizabeth, ones who are as bold as you."

She lifted her brilliant eyes to meet his gaze. "I am not your enemy, my lord."

Not yet.

The words leaped into his mind unbidden.

Not yet, as Allicia had not yet been his enemy when they married. He was certain of that, and always had been.

Without another word, he placed Elizabeth's hand on his arm and silently escorted her back to Donhallow.

That night, Elizabeth stood by the window in the bedchamber, toying with a loose bit of thread from the edge of her sleeve as she looked at the pale moon hanging in the sky over the castle walls. Stars, gleaming little points of light, twinkled in the blackness. Were they each of them alone, or were the constellations families of stars, banded together in love and harmony? It pleased her to think they were.

Would she ever be a part of a family again? Maybe if she could learn to hold her tongue and be an obedient, docile wife, as she had promised she would.

What if she couldn't? So far, she had not had much success. Perhaps Lord Kirkheathe was already planning to annul the marriage and send her back. Even though the marriage had been consummated, there were ways to do that. Five of the women at the convent had been sent there because their dissatisfied husbands had found some obscure blood tie that rendered their unions illegal.

She mustn't go back. As bad as it was before, it would be a thousand times worse after this taste of freedom…and other things.

She should have listened to Rual when she told her how Lord Kirkheathe felt about peddlers. Nevertheless, she was only trying to be charitable.

It was very disturbing to discover that her husband was, as her uncle had warned, not a kind-hearted man.

Had she not endured enough already? Was there to be no happiness for her, ever? Was she to always live in dread of pain and sharp, hateful words? Would she never have peace?

Perhaps once she was with child, they would not have much to do with one another.

No, that would not do, either. Even after so short a time as the lady of the castle, she knew she did not want her husband to ignore her. She wanted to be a wife, not a breeder of children. Besides, if he cared nothing for her, would he have come looking for her as he had, and warned her of danger?

And then there was the strange, haunted look that had come to his eyes when she had sworn she was not his enemy, almost as if he was afraid to believe her. Given what his first wife had tried to do, surely it was not so strange that he would be slow to trust her.

Perhaps she would just have to be patient.

She let her gaze follow the sentry on the wall walk. He marched to and fro, occasionally stopping to talk to his fellow guard, but not for long. Her husband's men were clearly too well trained for any slackness in their duties.

She went to the door and listened. Did he intend to stay below in the hall with the men all night?

Not that he seemed to enjoy their company any more than he had hers this evening. He had said not a word to her after they returned to Donhallow from the village, not even during the evening meal. Afterward, he had tossed scraps to his dog and stared morosely at the fire.

She had been silent, too. That was easier here than at the convent, she had to admit, with the excellent food to feast on, yet this enforced lack of conversation added to her anxiety.

They were husband and wife. That didn't mean that they would always see eye-to-eye, and she had promised to defer to him, and she would try to be patient.

However, as her husband, did he not have obligations, too? Was she wrong to desire his respect, if not his affection?

Despite her bold thoughts, she scrambled under the covers as her husband's familiar footfalls sounded in the corridor, as well as the click of his huge dog's nails.

Pulling the coverings up under her chin, she watched as Cadmus entered and ran about the room, sniffing.

She frowned. If there was or had been an intruder here, she would already be dead. "There is no one here but me, my lord," she called out, her determination not to be a coward reasserting itself.

He entered, striding toward the washstand, while Cadmus sauntered toward the bed. She pulled her knees up to her chest and shifted to the center.

Her husband began his ablutions. "I told you, he will not bite."

"I wouldn't be surprised if Cadmus thinks I am an intruder."

As if to prove her wrong, the big brute laid his chin on the bed and stared at her with what looked like devotion.

Or maybe she was appetizing.

"His looks may be more fierce than his nature, but I have no way of being sure about what he might do," she continued. "I have not known him long."

Her husband slowly turned to look at her. She had

not been speaking of him but, she realized, he obviously thought she was.

That was a good plan.

Keeping the same matter-of-fact tone, she said, "It can be difficult to adjust to new people."

His brow furrowed slightly. "I suppose."

"And sometimes, without meaning to, mistakes can be made."

He regarded her for a long moment. "Years ago, a peddler brought a sickness here," he finally replied. "He arrived ill, and whatever upset the balance of his humors, it soon spread to others. My father and I, and many others, were laid low, the old and very young most of all. Several people died, including my father."

Elizabeth flushed. "I didn't know, my lord, or I would not have been so upset when you sent them away."

"Such men are often dishonest, too," he added. "I do not want my people cheated."

"I can comprehend that, too, and to speak truly, I can believe that peddler might not be the most honest of men. It was the woman and child I wanted to help."

"I could have explained to you instead of flying into a temper," he grudgingly conceded. "I did not know my wife would feel it so necessary to share our food."

"I was taught a chatelaine should dispense charity, my lord. In future, however, I shall ask first."

"Good."

He took off his belt and tossed it on the chest. Her heart began to race as he stripped off his tunic and laid it beside the belt, but she would not be distracted. "My lord, as you are my husband, I am bound to respect and honor you, and I shall ask before I am charitable. I apologize for causing any trouble. But I…" She took a deep breath. "I don't want to be afraid of you."

He stared at her a long moment.

Then, as he looked at her, it seemed as if something within him yielded. His expression softened— only a little, but enough to tell her that he meant what he said next. "I do not want you to fear me, either."

A strange sense of giddiness blanketed her, as it did the times she was nearly caught when she was stealing food, and escaped. "Then tell me, my lord, is it your nature to sulk?"

His brows lowered.

Fearing that she had ruined what she had just achieved with a flippant remark, words came tumbling out of her mouth in an attempt to dispel her dismay. "Or perhaps it is simply your nature to be surly in the evenings. If so, I will take up my needle and sew, as much as I dislike it. I always prick my fingers. Or I could learn to play chess, although it looks to be a boring game. I saw the Mother and one of the sisters play once, while I was scrubbing the floor of the nun's hall. They just sat and stared at the board, it seemed. I can be silent, if you would prefer that.''

One of his brows slowly rose.

''I *can* be quiet, if I must. The Lord knows I have had years to learn. I can more easily bear the silence if I know you are not purposefully ignoring me. I do not like to be ignored.''

A sparkle of amusement twinkled in his eye. ''I noticed.''

''Compared to *some* people,'' she went on as relief flooded through her. ''I may not have a quiet nature, but it has never been my way to seek attention simply for attention's sake. I did all I could to escape notice at the convent, but I was not very successful.''

''That I can believe.''

''I only want you to understand that I don't want you to ignore me when I have displeased you. I can learn from my errors, and I do remember the vow I made to you when you agreed to marry me.''

''Good.''

He sat on the bed and removed his boots, then rose and took off his breeches. As he looked at her, his body naked, his skin glowing in the candlelight, his savage hair about his shoulders, there was something else she would never forget: how he had taken her with such fierce passion in his solar that morning.

She swallowed hard. ''If you don't want to talk

to me, naturally I don't expect you to force yourself. As I said, I can keep quiet when I..."

He got in beside her. "Elizabeth, be quiet," he whispered in his low, husky voice as he pulled her into his arms and covered her mouth with his.

He kissed her with so much ardor, he took her breath away. As for speaking, there was not a thing she wanted to say as she returned his kiss with equal passion.

His strong arms held her tight as his tongue gently, but with the certainty that she would not refuse, slipped into her mouth.

With equally exquisite leisure and command he began to stroke her body. His fingers glided over her back, her breasts, her thighs with the same delicate touch a musician used to play a harp.

And how he made her body sing!

But she was not a passive thing, and she could not resist the urge to stroke and caress her husband's virile body. She felt every scar, and when her fingertips brushed across his hardened nipples, she gloried in his gasp of pleasure.

"Can we do it twice in one day?" she asked, her breathing fast and shallow as she stared into his darkly passionate eyes.

He pulled away a little. "Are you sore?"

"A little, but not much." She flushed with embarrassment, yet didn't look away. "I don't mind a little pain."

"I will make you ready for me this time," he vowed in a low, seductive rasp.

Her heart racing, she whispered, "How do you do that?"

"Like this."

Chapter Nine

Leaning his weight on one arm, Raymond reached toward Elizabeth's bare foot with his free hand, then ran his finger from the crevice between her toes toward her ankle and up her naked leg. She had never known such exquisite torment and she could not help squirming.

Then he started at the toes of the other foot, and as he dragged his fingers over her, he bent down to press light kisses on her neck. Then her collarbone. Then, through the light fabric of her shift, her breasts, that sensation making her feel as if something inside her was being drawn tighter and tighter and tighter.

He untied the knot in the drawstring of her shift and slipped his hand inside.

Gasping, she arched back, offering all of her body to him, anxious for his passionate embrace.

He moved, lifting himself so that he was kneeling between her legs, but he didn't enter her. Not yet.

Instead, he continued to kiss and caress her. His hands lightly swept over her, touching her in places nobody had ever touched her, and as tenderly as if she were a fine and expensive piece of glass.

"Love me, my lord," she moaned. "Please, love me."

He stilled, and she opened her eyes to find him gazing at her with a strange expression.

"What is it?" she cried, more afraid now than she had ever been, of his dog, or the Reverend Mother, or him. "What have I done?"

"You?" he replied so quietly she could scarcely hear him above the pounding of her own heart. His eyes shimmered in the candlelight as he brushed a strand of hair from her cheek. "You have done nothing."

"Should I? Is there something more I should do?" she asked, half eager, half shy, certain that there must be. She should surely participate more, or perhaps she had done something wrong.

Determined to prove that she could learn, she raised her hand and brushed her fingers over him, using that same light touch. Closing his eyes, he sucked in his breath.

She grabbed hold of his shoulders and pulled herself up so that she could suck his nipple between her teeth and tease it with her tongue.

As her lips explored his chest and she buried her hands in his long hair, he ground his hips against her, the weight adding to her excitement. Taking one hand, she pushed up her shift, then leaned back, pulling him down upon her with the other hand.

With a low and hungry growl, he took her again with fiery passion.

Gripping him, she turned her head and bit her lip to keep from crying out.

Not in ecstasy, but in distress.

She would say nothing to stop him, although this hurt more than she had anticipated. He was her husband and this was his right.

Fortunately, she did not have to brook the agony long. He cried out and relaxed, lying with his weight on his elbows, his breath hot and panting in her ear.

He raised himself higher and looked at her, frowning. "What is it?"

"It was a little painful, my lord."

He rolled onto his side and glared at her. "Why did you not tell me?"

"Because you are my husband."

"I don't want to hurt you."

"But if we are to make a baby…"

"I could have waited a day. Or more."

"Perhaps I could not. I want to bear you a child, my lord."

"So this is but a duty to be endured?"

She wished she knew him better, so she would say the right thing. "Do you want an honest answer, my lord, or a suitably ladylike one?"

His gaze searched her face. "The honest one."

"Then I confess that I would gladly endure the

hurt for what went before, even if that was not the way to make a baby.''

A smile slowly dawned on his face, and his pleased expression made her happy, too. "Come," he said softly, and this time, as he held one arm out for her to nestle beside him, it was not an order.

It was a request, and one Elizabeth was glad to obey.

Raymond felt something licking his fingers. "Cadmus," he chided sleepily, rolling over onto his back and pulling his hand under the covers.

"It was I, my lord."

Raymond opened his eyes wide and found Elizabeth standing beside the bed, fully clothed in that loathsome gray dress, her beautiful hair covered by a plain white scarf with a neat mend in the bottom of one corner, and a wimple about her elfin chin.

God's wounds, she was pretty and charming, with that shy smile coupled with her boldly searching eyes.

"You licked me?" he asked huskily, believing she might do something so outrageous, and outrageously exciting.

"I kissed your hand," she replied, her smile widening in a way that he found totally beguiling.

Wrapping his hand around her neck, he drew her down to press a kiss onto her soft, firm lips. "Come back to bed."

She pulled away. "It is after dawn, my lord."

He glanced at the window and regretfully realized she was right.

"I have not been awake long," she said.

He raised his eyebrows.

"Very well. I awoke before dawn—but you watched me sleep yesterday. I thought today I would watch you. Do you know you look much younger when you sleep?"

Younger and more vulnerable, perhaps?

She was not Allicia, and as he had said last night, *she* had done nothing to warrant his suspicions.

Neither had Allicia, until he felt the leather strap tightening around his neck.

"Have I said something wrong? I didn't mean to imply that there was anything bad about the way you look when you are awake."

That brought a smile to his lips. "How are you?" he asked.

"Not very sore."

A surge of desire flashed through him, powerful and primitive. However, as he had said last night, he could be patient. He really ought to let her body get used to him.

He climbed out of the bed and her eyes widened. He did not explain that a man need not be aroused to be in that state first thing in the morning, although at present, he was.

"Rual tells me you have no steward, either of the estate or the household," she said after he had pulled on his breeches.

He nodded.

She sat on the bed and watched him dress. "That must make a lot of work for you, managing both the castle and your tenants besides. I should think a man of your wealth and station should have at least an estate steward, or do you have them to run your other estates?"

She would find this out soon enough, he reasoned.

"I have no other estates."

"None?"

"None."

"But my uncle impiied—" She fell silent, her forehead wrinkled.

He hoped she didn't ask about his money.

"Well, one large estate is better than several small ones. We would have to be traveling from one to the other all the time. How large is your estate, my lord?"

"Large enough." *Larger than Montross's, at any rate.*

She twisted her fingers in her lap. "I don't mean to pry."

He kept silent as he put on his sword belt.

"Will you ride out again today?"

He inclined his head in assertion.

"Do you patrol because of serious trouble, my lord? Do you expect an attack, although I must say I am shocked anybody would dare."

His lips jerked up into a smile. "They would if they thought they could." She rose and came toward him, an enticing, powerfully seductive softness in her eyes.

"We also look for thieves or poachers," he continued, his low voice falling softly. "Check the state of the roads and byways. Many things."

"If any man tried to attack you or your castle, he would be a fool," she whispered as she ran her hands up his chest.

With a great sense of self-restraint, he grabbed them and looked down at her. "Stop, or you may never heal."

She pouted, her bottom lip thrust out in a manner that nearly made him forget what he had just said. Instead, he chucked her lightly under the chin. "Now who is sulking?"

She laughed softly as she embraced him around the waist. It was a gesture at once familiar and pleasant. "I cannot help but be disappointed, my lord. I want to bear your child so much!"

"A child or *my* child?"

A sincere smile lit her face. "Yours, my Lord Kirkheathe. Yours."

His lips found hers in an instant. Holding her close, he wanted to forget the memories and all the suspicion it created within him. He wished that the past could be wiped away and he could be born anew, able to love without dread and trust her completely. Perhaps some day...

Cadmus whined at the door and he reluctantly stopped kissing her.

"I think he wants to go out," Elizabeth observed with a mischievous gleam in her eyes. "I should eat, too. To keep up my strength."

Chuckling softly, he went to the door and let Cadmus out, then waited for her to take his arm to go to the chapel for mass.

"May I ride with you on your patrol?"

He halted on the tower steps and looked at her questioningly.

Her eyes shone eagerly. "Cadmus is not the only one who has been inside too long. The journey here was the first time I was outside the walls of the convent in thirteen years, and yesterday the first time I have felt free for long before that. I would very much like to see your estate, too, if I may. It looks to be a fine day, and I think I am not too sore."

Why not? Why not let her ride out with him? And yet, if he gave in to her request, what kind of precedent would he be setting? "You were not going to ask for anything."

"Oh," she said, lowering her head so that he couldn't see her beautiful eyes. "I forgot again, didn't I? I'm sorry, my lord," she finished sadly.

What she asked was a small thing, and cost nothing. Surely it was not worth making her sad. Besides, the tenants should see his bride, as the villagers had.

His beautiful, bold bride. Pride swelled within him, as it had when he had seen the envy in Montross's eyes. "You may come."

She raised her head, but she was not happier. "Perhaps it would be better for me to stay here."

"I said you may come."

"Is that an order, my lord?"

Confounded, he shook his head. "I would like it."

She swiped at her eyes. God's rood, was she wiping away tears?

He took her by the shoulders and gazed at her intently, seeking confirmation.

She didn't meet his gaze. "If I embarrass you, my lord, I am content to stay here."

Embarrass him? How? By being the most beautiful, spirited and passionate wife he could hope for? "You do not."

She continued to stare at the floor—or her garments?

Of course, that had to be it. She was ashamed of her clothes. He would buy her some new ones with some of her dower money. Surely they could spare enough for that.

"I am not ashamed of you," he assured her.

Swiftly, she raised her head, her splendid eyes shining with both doubt and hope. "You're not?"

"No."

"Then I shall be delighted to ride out with you," she said, putting her arm through his. "Provided you have a gentle mare and do not intend to go very fast. You may recall, my lord, that I am a little sore."

* * *

"I am pleased to think there is such a large wood on your estate, my lord," Elizabeth observed as she rode beside him on an exceptionally placid mare.

Her breath looked like puffs of smoke in the chill January air, but above them, the sky was a brilliant winter blue. No snow lay upon the ground, and in the sunlight, it seemed almost spring.

"I confess that when we approached your castle from the west, it seemed set in a very barren place."

Instead, as she now knew, to the south and east there was a wood of both size and variety. And, as she had foreseen, it was a beautiful day.

She was as happy as she had ever been as she rode proudly beside her husband under the cover of the trees, with the men behind and nobody else watching.

She had come to realize that when she was at Donhallow, everybody watched her. She was used to being the center of attention, but for her sins. In that case, the other girls had glanced at her surreptitiously, some in sympathy, others hoping to catch her doing more wrong.

To be sure, it was not like that at Donhallow. When she caught people's gaze there, *they* flushed and bowed and looked away as if they were the sinners, except Rual. She always met Elizabeth's gaze frankly, which pleased Elizabeth, Lady Katherine's edict regarding overfamiliarity with the servants notwithstanding.

It had occurred to Elizabeth today that Lady Katherine had never seemed a happy woman. Nevertheless, rumors had lately come to the convent via a new girl that Lady Katherine was married. That didn't seem possible, given her stern nature, and Elizabeth wondered what kind of man could possibly have conquered her former foster mother's heart. A man as stern as Lord Kirkheathe, perhaps.

Glancing at her grave husband beside her, she suddenly felt quite close to Lady Katherine, and wished her happy in her marriage.

Up ahead, a rabbit dashed into the middle of the rutted road, sat up and stared as if not believing anybody would have the audacity to interrupt its progress, then darted into the underbrush. As Elizabeth laughed, Cadmus gave a loud bark and loped off after it.

"I hope he doesn't catch that fine fellow," she said. "It would be a pity for him to wind up in a pot."

"It is a dog's nature to catch rabbits," her husband replied.

"I think that one may escape such a fate," she proposed. "He is very fast."

"A rabbit belongs in a pot."

"And Cadmus will catch him without fail?"

"Cadmus is a good hunter."

"I daresay you are, as well. Yet you did not bring your hawks."

"We do not hunt today," her husband replied.

"Except for Cadmus."

"Yes, except for Cadmus."

They continued on in companionable silence, and as they did, Elizabeth realized how free and happy she felt.

And how she wished the Reverend Mother could see her now.

Her present joy nearly made up for all her past suffering, and might have entirely, if this talk of hunting did not make her think of food. Food reminded her of the girls she had left behind. Hopefully one of them would take her place stealing food for the little ones.

Then she had an idea, one that grew stronger the more she thought about it. If her husband proved amenable, she would write to the bishop in charge of the convent, detailing the deprivations the girls suffered, despite the money sent for their welfare by their families. Surely the bishop would have to pay attention to the wife of Lord Kirkheathe.

She should have thought of this sooner, and not selfishly put her own concerns first.

"Are you uncomfortable?"

"Me? No, my lord. I was…thinking."

"Deeply," he agreed gravely.

"May we stop for a moment? In truth, I think a little respite from the saddle would not be amiss. And if there is a stream nearby, a drink of water would be welcome, too."

He nodded and raised his hand. The troop of men

halted their mounts. He threw his leg easily over the back of his large stallion and slid to the ground, then reached up and put his strong hands about her waist to help her down.

As she slipped along his body, heat flooded through her, even though the breeze was cool.

Looking into his dark eyes, she did not think she alone was affected by their proximity.

At that moment, though, Cadmus came bounding toward them through the underbrush, his tongue lolling as he panted, and no bleeding carcass in his mouth.

"He got away," she murmured with satisfaction. "I thought he looked clever."

"The rabbit?"

"Aye, my lord. The rabbit."

Raymond made a sound between a laugh and a bark, then turned to his waiting men.

"Stay here," he ordered before taking her gloved hand in his. "Stay," he commanded his dog, in exactly the same tone.

Blushing, Elizabeth glanced over her shoulder at the soldiers as he led her into the bushes. "Heaven only knows what they think we're doing, my lord."

"They heard you ask for water."

"I hope so. Or perhaps I should be flattered they might think you cannot stay away from me for even half a day."

He made that same bark of a laugh and his grip tightened as he led her farther into the wood.

Maybe he *was* thinking of doing more than drinking, and the sight of a ruined hut a little way in the distance made that seem a definite possibility—until he stopped in front of a babbling stream. "Drink."

She knelt on the bank and cupped her hands to bring the clear, cold water to her lips. Her thirst slaked, she twisted her head to look up at him—and saw blatant desire on his face. She swallowed hard as she wiped her lips with the back of her hand. "Are you...are you not thirsty, my lord?"

He shook his head.

"Hungry, perhaps?"

He slowly smiled.

"Me, too," she whispered as she got to her feet. "Even though my belly is full."

His eyes gleamed.

There might never be a better time. "But the girls I left behind at the convent are starving. Do you think, my lord, that I could write to the bishop and tell him so? I'm sure the Reverend Mother is well paid in her charge of them and keeps most of the money for herself. Unfortunately, visitors are very rare and the girls are not allowed to write, even if they know how. Now that I am free—and gratefully so, I assure you—it would be selfish of me to do nothing. I must help them if I can. They may not be so fortunate as to be married some day, many of them, and it is a harsh..." In light of his expression, her words trailed off.

"Another request?"

"I do not ask for myself, my lord, but for them. If I forget them, it will be to my shame."

"Then write."

"Oh, thank you, my lord!" she cried, throwing her arms around him and laying her head against his chest. "You are most generous."

"It may not help."

Feeling the coarseness of his wool tunic against her cheek as she raised her face, she said, "But it may. At least the Reverend Mother will know that I do not intend to keep quiet about her management of the convent."

Although his features softened a bit, he pulled away from her. "You, keep quiet?"

She thought of her happy exclamations as they rode along. "Do I talk too much for your taste, my lord? I *can* be quiet, if that will suit you better."

"No, it will not."

She sighed with relief.

"Tell me about her."

"The Reverend Mother?" she said with honest revulsion. "I would rather not."

"Then the other girls."

"There is not much to tell. We didn't get much chance to talk, so when I say I can keep quiet, believe it, my lord. We went whole weeks without speaking. And we were not to talk when we were in our sleeping quarters, or at work, or at mass or at table."

He tilted his head.

"Yes, it was difficult for me. That was one reason I was punished, too. I tried to whisper, but they always caught me. I was much more successful stealing food."

"How?"

"How did they catch me, or how did they punish me?"

"Punish you."

"By whipping me, as you already know from the scars. And making me fast and keep vigils. Oh, and scrubbing floors—they knew I hated it. The cold water, kneeling on the stones...I tell you, my lord, there were days I thought my knees would never stop aching."

"Go on."

"There is no more to tell, not about that place. I would much rather talk of other things."

"As you wish."

"Should we not be getting back to the others?"

"They can wait."

Chapter Ten

Lord Kirkheathe went to a fallen tree nearby and sat on the trunk. He gestured for Elizabeth to join him.

When she did, she talked with a freedom she had not known in a long time. She told him of her parents and their untimely deaths, of the years being shunted from relative to relative, of her short, yet pleasant, time with the stern Lady Katherine Du-Monde. "You know, my lord, she was quite a bit like you, except that she was a woman, of course. Very stern and a great believer of discipline."

For the first time since they had sat upon the log, her husband spoke. "Discipline?"

"Yes, I know you insist upon it, too. Your men are very well-trained, certainly better than my uncle's. The two times we stopped at an inn on the way here, they would go off and gamble and drink and sport, and he would have a terrible time rounding them up again. If I had not been so afraid of what lay ahead, it would have been quite amusing."

"You think me stern?"

"You cannot deny that, but," she murmured, placing her hand on his arm, "I am beginning to realize, not all the time. Not when we are alone, like this." She cocked her head to regard him with an affection that was growing deeper every time they were together. "You were going to kiss me before, I think, my lord."

He lifted one side of his mouth in a wry smile, then got to his feet and held out his hand. "The men have been waiting a long time."

"Oh," she said as she placed her hand in his and rose.

Then, suddenly, he yanked her to him and kissed her with so much heated passion, she felt dizzy.

"Besides, you are sore," he whispered as his lips trailed over her cheek toward her neck and she arched her back.

"I...I am feeling better. Can't the men wait a little longer?"

"No." He stepped away and she could have groaned with frustration and disappointment. His eyes sparkled as he took her hand to lead her back the way they had come. "You look bereft."

"My lord, you cannot kiss me like that and then expect me to be calm, or not wanting more."

"Good."

She halted and he had to stop, too. "I think you

are a rogue, my lord. A very tempting one, to be sure, but a rogue nonetheless.''

Rogue? No, he was a devil, if his seductive little smile was anything to judge by. ''When you are not sore, you will see what kind of rogue I can be.''

She had to clear her throat. ''Perhaps tonight, my lord?''

''Whenever you are ready.''

''Or perhaps we do not have to do *all* we did last night,'' she suggested hopefully.

''And you were not going to ask for things,'' he chided softly as with a low chuckle, he gathered her into his arms.

The men had to wait somewhat longer.

''It can't be true,'' Fane Montross muttered several days later as he glared at the woman. He picked up a piece of daub that had fallen from the decrepit hut's crumbling walls and threw it across the small interior toward what had once been the hearth. ''How can she even like that cretin?''

Rual shrugged. ''How do I know? What I do know is, she's falling in love with him, despite what you think, and I think him with her, too.''

''How do you know?''

''Because I have eyes in my head, and it's that plain. I've been keeping a close eye on them since she came, and I tell you, he's different. Almost...mellow.''

Fane snorted. "Raymond mellow? That I would pay to see."

"Do you doubt me?" Rual charged.

"No. I shall take your word for it."

"And she's like a besotted girl with a secret lover. Makes me sick to look at them."

"She has no idea you loathe him?"

"Am I a fool? Of course not."

"And no idea who you are...or rather, who your family was?"

"The earl thought we were all dead when he stole our land and got the king to give D'Estienne my father's title."

"Your father was a traitor."

"But was my mother? Was I, his daughter? There was no reason for the king to take away our livelihood."

"Except the law, Rual. All a traitor's property is forfeit to the crown. I confess I am surprised you ever bothered to come back."

"Don't trouble yourself to spout the law to me, Sir Fane. I know it better than you. And why should I not return? I have more right to be here than Raymond D'Estienne, and I will get justice in my own way."

"I would take care how you speak to me, woman. I could kill you right now with no repercussions and no remorse. Your body would be found in the woods, and they would blame thieves or gypsies. Never me."

Rual's lips curved up into a smile. "You could, but then you'd have no spy in Donhallow. Everybody else in there thinks the man walks on water, or they're terrified of him."

"Tell me, Rual, why don't you kill him yourself?"

"To be hung? As much as I hate him and all his family, I value my life."

"You could be discovered to be a spy. Are you sure Kirkheathe has no suspicions?"

"None."

"You'll never get the estate back, even when he's dead," he observed.

"I know that, too," she snapped. "But for now, I will help his enemy destroy him and make a pretty penny out of it, too."

"Indeed you will." Fane held out the purse of silver coins. "With all I pay you, you could go to London and live like a queen."

"I won't leave here until he's dead," she mumbled as she snatched the purse.

"Still, quite a risk you're taking."

"It's worth it," she said, shaking the bags of coins. "As you said, I can go to London and live like a queen when he's dead."

"And he will be soon enough, I promise you. Plans are already in motion. Lots of things can happen when a man travels from home."

"Aye, I know," Rual said slyly.

He suddenly lunged at her and grabbed her by the throat. "And you had better keep your mouth shut."

"I will," she gasped, her eyes wide as she vainly tried to pull his hands off her.

"See that you do," he snarled as he shoved her away. "Now take your money and get back before you're missed."

Raymond kept the smile of satisfaction off his face as he rolled up the parchment message bearing the seal of the earl of Chesney. "Tell him I shall be pleased to attend," he said to the messenger who had brought the scroll and now waited for his response.

The nervous young man bowed. "As it pleases you, my lord."

"You will stay the night and return in the morning."

"Thank you, my lord."

"You may go."

The youth was only too keen to depart the solar.

Raymond rose and went to the window to look out over his castle. At last, the earl, his overlord, had asked him to attend his council. Raymond had lived on this estate all his life, yet never once had the earl deigned to ask him, or his father, to council.

Coming so soon after Raymond's marriage, the reason for the change was all too plain. It was because of his marriage to a niece of Lord Perronet, long a friend and ally of the earl's.

Montross would not be pleased. The sly and charming Montross had had the earl's ear for years, but now perhaps that influence was on the wane. Another reason, Raymond told himself, he was pleased that he had taken Elizabeth for his wife.

However, despite what he had thought when he agreed to the marriage, the alliance with Perronet was not the most important reason for his pleasure now.

Beautiful, bold, loving Elizabeth was.

He delighted in her company whenever she was near, and especially when they were alone—and not necessarily in bed. Just having her nearby was a delight, to see her vivacious face and hear her lovely voice, to have her glance at him with her bright, approving eyes. To know that he could bring a smile to her face, and she to his, and that this amazing, wonderful woman was his wife.

She made him feel fully a man again, not a monster with an ogre's voice who frightened men, women and children.

She was likely in the kitchen at present, discussing the plans for the week's meals. Although she always ate with gusto and appreciation for the cook's efforts—something that was putting some necessary flesh on her thin limbs—she was a frugal woman. He was grateful for that, he thought as he turned to go below. Otherwise, she might be emptying his purse more quickly than he would have liked.

Well, in one way, she already was, although she did not know it. He was spending too much money on her. She had needed new clothes, and although the ones he had purchased for her were plain enough, he had used a sum he really couldn't spare. Despite that, he did not regret it, for she had been as grateful for them as she had been the morning he had let her stay abed.

Her gratitude was very pleasant, too.

The earl's castle was at the center of a large town, he reflected as he strode out of his solar. Perhaps he could buy her a pretty gown, one in red or green to set off her complexion or her eyes.

Or perhaps he should buy her a harp. He didn't have to go to Chesney for that; there was Johannes in the village—but then it might not be a surprise.

He very much enjoyed surprising her, watching her eyes light up and her smile blossom.

Yes, he would definitely buy her a harp, and maybe a gown, too.

He entered the hall, glancing about quickly to see who was there. Elizabeth was near the hearth, seated on the bench, the young messenger beside her.

Not so very young, that messenger, Raymond realized. About her age. And he was good-looking, too, in a soft sort of way, like Montross.

Worst of all, Elizabeth was laughing at something the messenger had said.

In a few long strides that made his tunic whip about his ankles, Raymond stood before them.

The messenger jumped to his feet, startled and turning pale. Elizabeth's brow furrowed questioningly, and, as she glanced at the messenger, she made a little frown. "Yes, my lord?"

"Come with me."

"Of course," she replied calmly. "Excuse me, Douglas."

The young man bowed stiffly.

Raymond spun on his heel and returned to their solar. Once there, he waited for Elizabeth, who entered a few moments later, slightly out of breath. "Whatever is the matter?" she asked. "What has happened?"

"I am invited to Chesney, to confer with the earl."

Her eyes widened. "That is bad?"

He shook his head.

"It is good?"

He nodded.

"Oh," she sighed, sitting down in the nearest chair. "I was afraid it was something terrible. You certainly acted as if it were. You frightened me half to death."

He hadn't meant to do that. The messenger, perhaps, but not her.

She continued to regard him. "What else? There is something more. Is it...I am not to go with you, am I?"

"No."

"Will you be away long?"

"A few days."

"While I do not enjoy the thought of your absence, my lord, I confess I am a little relieved," she admitted. "I am still not used to the deference accorded a lord's wife."

He walked to the window and looked out at the sky. "You seemed to enjoy it a moment ago," he growled.

To his surprise and annoyance, she laughed and said, "I did."

He whirled around and glared at her, and at once, she sobered. "My lord," she asked, rising, "what have I done? I merely spoke with the earl's messenger and yes, I admit that after my days at the convent where I was treated little better than a leper by most of the nuns, I will confess I am pleased to be deferred to a little, but that does not mean I feel comfortable with it." She approached him warily. "If the earl is not your enemy, what harm is there in my being pleasant to his emissary?"

He clenched his jaw and turned away again.

She took him by the shoulders, forcing him to look at her. "How is that wrong?"

"I didn't like the way he looked at you."

"The way he...?" Obviously bewildered, she dropped her hands and drew back. "He was merely being polite."

"You were laughing together."

"He said he found you most intimidating, and I said, so did I. Then I laughed, and he relaxed and laughed, too. It is a chatelaine's duty to make her guests comfortable. I see no harm in what I said, or in laughing.''

He didn't answer, and after an instant while her gaze anxiously searched his face, sudden realization dawned in her eyes, along with disbelief. ''My lord, are you…can you possibly be *jealous?*''

He strode toward the door. He wouldn't explain himself to her. He didn't have to. He was her husband, and it was for her to—

She ran in front of him and barred the door. ''You are jealous of that boy?'' she asked incredulously.

''Out of my way.''

''Not until you tell me the truth.''

He was very tempted to lie.

''It is true,'' she murmured incredulously. ''Good heavens, I cannot believe it. That is ridiculous!''

''You are my wife.''

''Yes, I am—one who is no beauty or exceptional in any way.''

''Stop being modest,'' he growled.

''I'm not, nor am I vain,'' she declared. ''Will you next tell me Cadmus is a beauty, too? Or is it merely that I am yours, and so must be cold and distant to all? If that is what you expect, I shall strive to obey—but it is most certainly not the way I was taught a lady should behave.

''Nor am I pleased that you would think I would take the sacrament of marriage lightly.'' She straightened her slender shoulders. ''If that is why you were so abrupt in the hall, you owe me an apology.''

''Apology?''

A look of utter resolve appeared in her eyes. ''I want you to listen to me, my lord, and mark these words. I will never dishonor you. I have made a vow before God to be your faithful wife, and so I shall be.''

He nodded. Yes, she was the kind who would abide by a sacred vow, no matter how tempted otherwise.

But if he did not have her heart, it didn't matter if she did not actually disgrace him. As he looked at her, with her passionate determination, defending her honor as vigorously as any warrior, he knew life without her love would be like a feast set before a man who could not taste it.

''I am an honorable woman, if not a pretty one.''

''Wait here.''

Without lingering to hear her answer, he left the solar and took the stairs to their bedchamber two at a time. He went to his large chest and, after throwing it open, burrowed deep inside, tossing out clothing and linen until he found the mirror he had put there years ago, when he could no longer bear to look at the scar around his neck.

He fished it out and just as swiftly returned to the solar, where she was still sitting. He held the mirror out to her.

She didn't move. ''What is it?''

"A mirror."

Her lip started to tremble. "Please don't do this to me, my lord. Please don't humiliate me this way."

He shoved the framed mirror into her hand, but she turned her head away and closed her eyes.

"Look," he commanded. He repeated the order, more softly this time. "Look at yourself, Elizabeth."

She pressed her lips together and obeyed.

Then, slowly, her eyes widened and her mouth fell open. "That is...why, that cannot be me," she murmured.

"It is."

She put her hand to her cheek wonderingly. "How is it possible?" she whispered. "It could almost be my cousin Genevieve staring back at me. My uncle wasn't lying, after all."

To his surprise, she didn't look happy. She looked miserable.

"The Reverend Mother always called me ugly, and nobody contradicted her. And of course, there were no mirrors at the convent."

She raised her sorrowful eyes to look at him. "Why did she always tell me I was ugly?"

"To hurt you," he replied gently. "And to break your spirit."

"I almost wish you hadn't shown me," she said, giving him back the mirror, her hand trembling. "I feel...I am so confused. When the villagers and your men and Montross looked at me as they did, I thought their attention was only because I was your wife. I had no notion it had anything to do with the way I look. That it could. I am the same person inside, but to know..." Her words trailed off.

She sat so still, her hands loose in her lap, it was as if something within her had died.

God's wounds, shouldn't a woman be glad to realize she was beautiful? "What troubles you?"

"Is that why you accepted me as your bride, my lord?" she whispered, her face full of anguish. "Is that why you make love with me as you do, because I am pretty?"

He knelt beside her, taking her smaller hands in his. "Remember the first time we were together? It was not as our other nights have been."

Not meeting his gaze, she nodded.

"You looked then as you do now."

At last she raised her eyes.

"You are much more than a pretty woman, Elizabeth."

"I...I am?"

He wiped a tear from her cheek. "Very much more."

She smiled tremulously. "I am glad, my lord, to hear you say it. I was so afraid."

He couldn't comprehend that. Elizabeth afraid? She was the boldest, bravest woman he had ever met.

"Everything I understood about the way people

responded to me has been based upon a lie, and I admit I was delighted to think that you found merit in me despite my lack of beauty. Imagine, then, my horror to think that perhaps it was nothing more than that, after all.'' She sighed and reached out to caress his cheek. ''But you, I think, can understand better than most that I still want things to be as they were. I had an idea of the world, and my place in it as a homely woman, just as you had an idea of the world and your place in it before your trust was betrayed and your voice ruined.

''How difficult it must have been for you! I am upset, and what I have learned should be pleasing. You had to deal with something so much worse. I cannot imagine how it must have been for you. It must have been shattering.''

Oh, God.

He closed his eyes and silently offered a fervent thanks to heaven for sending him Elizabeth, who could understand what he had endured and how his world had altered.

''And I think you loved her, too.''

Ever since Allicia's betrayal, he had tried to forget that he had ever felt that way about her. He had been too full of despair and fear and anger to admit even to himself that he had once cared about her.

Yet now, hearing someone else say those words, something seemed to break within him, and a wall of constraint he had built around his heart crumbled.

''Oh, God, how I loved her,'' he said, his voice choking as he laid his head in Elizabeth's lap.

Chapter Eleven

Elizabeth put her arms about Raymond and held him close. As she stroked his hair, she realized she had never thought a man could experience heartache as a woman could.

But now she knew that was wrong. Raymond bore the weight of loss and betrayal and a permanent physical reminder of those things. He was not an unfeeling collection of bone and muscle and sinew. And had she not been learning just how loving he could be? A man who could love as he did could be terribly hurt by that emotion, too.

What had she suffered compared to him?

And yet, to hear him admit that he had loved another...

She must not begrudge him that.

And then he raised his head and fixed his dark-eyed gaze upon her face. "I loved her because she was beautiful. Because I was proud she accepted me. But there was always something... I know now I did not love her for herself, Elizabeth. Not as I love you.''

She stared a moment, afraid to believe what he was saying.

''I mean it, Elizabeth. I never cared for her as I do you. She never made me as happy as you do, and she would never have accepted a man with a ruined voice like mine.''

''Oh, Raymond,'' she cried softly, joy filling her as she once again held him close.

They stayed thus for a long moment, until she reluctantly pulled away. ''Shall we return to the hall, my lord?'' she asked. ''That poor messenger may fear he is in deep trouble, or that I am.''

''Not yet,'' he said, getting to his feet.

''I must say I am pleased to think you don't have to be ashamed of your wife's face. I thought perhaps Montross was pitying you for that. That is one reason I was so bold in the courtyard that day, and why I was afraid I had offended you.''

''I liked it.''

''You didn't just tolerate it?''

His lips jerked up in a smile. ''No.''

''If I had known I was pretty, I wouldn't have been so afraid. I might have been even more impertinent and really given your enemy cause to envy you.''

''He does.''

''I am glad.''

"I hope you will not fear me ever again, Elizabeth."

"I don't think I could now," she confessed, rising and putting her arms lightly about his waist as she gave him a wry, sidelong glance. "But I would not want to damage your reputation, my lord. Perhaps I should pretend to tremble when you come near me?"

He stroked her cheek. "There is only one reason I would have you tremble, Elizabeth."

"What might that be, my lord?"

His smile grew.

As heat spilled through her, she made a great sigh. "I am going to miss you when you go to Chesney."

"The invitation is only to me."

"As long as I must stay behind not because you think I will flirt with other men at the earl's castle, or otherwise act like a vain and silly girl. Believe me, my lord, I have had my fill of them."

"I will miss you, too."

She smiled up at him, delighted and thrilled by his sincere words. "There is some time before the evening meal," she noted with feigned nonchalance.

"Elizabeth?"

"Yes, my lord?"

"Come with me to our bedchamber."

"What about the messenger?"

He gave her a wry grin. "Very well, we shall return to the hall and assuage the young man's dread."

"I really think we should."

"*Then* we shall go to our chamber."

Her warm, seductive laughter filled the solar. "As you command, my lord."

Raymond's gaze swept over the assembled nobles in the great hall of Chesney Castle. Never before, except in London, had he been among so many.

He also marveled at the size and luxurious furnishings in the earl's hall. It was very obvious he was a man of vast wealth, and that meant power, too.

Yet Raymond was here by invitation, not command. That was a heady feeling. Still, that was not what was really pleasing him this morning. It was the thought of the harp he had purchased for Elizabeth yesterday, the very day they had arrived. He had also found some lovely fabric for a cloak for her, and fox furs to line it.

There was another item whose recollection made him want to grin from ear to ear: a silk shift. To be sure, it had cost him dear, but when he had imagined the soft, thin fabric caressing Elizabeth's body, he had been unable to resist purchasing it.

He had also been seriously tempted to ride for home at once with his presents.

"Lord Kirkheathe, what a delightful surprise," a familiar voice murmured in his ear.

He turned to find Elizabeth's uncle at his elbow. "Lord Perronet."

The man surreptitiously studied him. "How is my niece?"

"Well."

"With child?"

"It has been only a month, my lord," Raymond reminded him.

Perronet flushed. "Oh, yes, of course." He cleared his throat. "She is...that is, you do not find her...?"

"She suits me." That was a pale description of how Elizabeth made him feel, but good enough to satisfy Perronet, who breathed a heavy sigh of relief and said, "Oh, there is the earl of Lockington. I have something to discuss with him. Farewell until later, my lord."

Raymond inclined his head and thankfully watched him go.

"As God is my hope, it's Raymond D'Estienne!"

Another familiar voice, but this was one to make Raymond smile. He waited as Baron Clarewood hurried toward him with his customary speed. "I am delighted to see you, my friend."

The baron came to a halt and smiled broadly, yet with a hint of concern in his pleasant brown eyes. "Are you here by command or invitation?"

Raymond smiled. "Invitation."

"Splendid—and about time, too!" Charles declared. "But now tell me, is it true? Have you married again at last?"

It had always been Charles's way to be blunt,

even in his youth, and Raymond took no offense at his question, or its form. "Yes."

"And to Perronet's niece?"

Raymond nodded.

"Splendid again. What is she like?"

Raymond pondered a moment, wondering if there were words to truly do justice to Elizabeth. In view of his friend's growing impatience, he responded with a wider smile and said, "She suits me."

Charles grinned. "God in Heaven, a miracle!"

"One could say so."

"What does she look like?" Charles demanded, glancing at Perronet.

"Not like her uncle."

"God be praised for that! And she's done you good. I can see that right off. Wonderful, my friend, wonderful!" he declared, clapping Raymond on the shoulder with a familiarity that caught the attention of several men nearby.

Charles saw them looking, too. "Come over here, where we can be more private," he urged. "Five years I haven't seen you," he chided when they got to a more secluded corner. "And you might have invited me to the wedding. Well, no matter," he went on without letting Raymond answer. "A fine match it is, without a doubt. Her cousin's married into the DeLanyea family, you know."

"I had heard she was married, yes," Raymond agreed, not begrudging the loss of her for an instant.

"So that means you are tied to one of the most

famous and popular families in the Marches. Half
Welsh they may be, but they are well regarded.
Great friends of Urien Fitzroy they are, too, the finest trainer of fighting men in England. My own boy
Alexander is nearly finished his time with him. If
anybody could give that boy some discipline, it'll
be Fitzroy. That's all the lad lacked. I say it though
he is my own son, Alexander has the best aim of
anyone I've ever met. If he can see a target, he can
hit it. But not a jot of self-discipline. Well, at least
he didn't have any. I daresay he does now.''

As Charles rambled on, Raymond could almost
taste the desire to have a son, too, and with Elizabeth
for a mother, he would surely be a son to be proud
of.

''This marriage also ties you to Baron De-
Guerre,'' Charles observed, pulling Raymond out of
his momentary reverie. ''What, you didn't know?
Didn't Perronet brag of the relations you would be
getting?''

''Not of DeGuerre.''

''Perhaps because Perronet doesn't think much of
upstarts, and Baron DeGuerre was born a bastard.''

''My own father was not nobly born,'' Raymond
reminded Charles. ''He was rewarded for good and
faithful service.''

''With another man's estate.''

''With a traitor's forfeited property.''

''Yes, well, that was long ago, and no one can
deny that you and your father have served the earl
well. And now that you're related to the DeLanyeas

by marriage, you're also tied to Baron DeGuerre, a most formidable fellow. Indeed, they are all important men, so it is no wonder to me you were invited here, Raymond. Montross must have soiled himself when he heard. I'm not surprised he didn't come.''

Fane Montross wasn't there? To Raymond's chagrin, he hadn't noticed this, and he should have.

''He sent word he is ill, but I don't believe it. Or maybe he is—sick that you've made such important connections.'' Charles's expression changed. ''Why, Raymond, I thought you would be pleased.''

Pleased? He was here, and Elizabeth was at home, and so was Fane Montross.

Elizabeth knew his feelings about Montross, and the reason for them. She was an intelligent woman who clearly had no liking for Montross, either. Surely she would take care.

Raymond had brought only a small troop with him. The rest he had left behind under Barden's command to protect his castle. Montross would be a fool to attack, especially now that Raymond had risen in the earl of Chesney's estimation.

It was not Montross's way to attack directly. He would use subtlety and subterfuge, which was why it might be true that he was too ill to attend here. Otherwise, Montross would have come and used the opportunity to speak against Raymond with other nobles, in private meetings. If he thought Raymond was getting too close to the earl, he would be here asserting his position as the more favored, and striving to ensure that it was so.

Unless he felt he had a more important reason for staying home.

Montross would know that Elizabeth was left behind. The villagers and tenants along the road had seen them ride out with baggage in tow.

If Montross dared to set foot on his land when he was not there…if he tried to visit the castle…if he touched so much as Elizabeth's hand, having come to Donhallow on some pretense of business knowing Raymond was away…

"Goodbye, Charles. I must go home."

"Go? But you have not yet made your obeisance to the earl," his friend protested. "To leave now could be misconstrued as an insult, or perhaps even treason since the earl represents the crown."

"I will make my apologies later."

"When?"

"I will send him a letter if not return myself."

"Montross wouldn't dare—"

"We cannot know what that man might dare."

"Raymond, this is foolishness! You have waited years for this and—"

"If the earl asks, tell him pressing business calls me home." Raymond clasped his friend by the forearm. "I cannot stay. Farewell, my friend."

"My lady?"

Elizabeth poked her head out of the buttery where

she had been counting the butts of ale intended for the servants. Raymond had been gone only a few days, but it was as if the essence of Donhallow had gone with him, leaving it half empty. The days dragged, so to while away the time, she busied herself with any and every task she could think of.

There was also another distraction, but she kept that to herself, and would until he returned.

"Yes?" she said to Rual.

"There is a woman here, my lady, who says she must speak to you."

Elizabeth stepped out from the buttery and wiped her hands on her makeshift apron. "A woman?"

"She says she is Erick's mother and that she needs your help."

Elizabeth had been thinking of the peddler's family often over the past days and wondering how they fared. "I'll see her at once. Where is she?"

"At the gatehouse. She will not come any farther."

Understandable after the way her husband had ordered them to leave, Elizabeth thought as she tore off her apron and handed it to Rual.

"You are going to speak with her?" Rual asked warily.

"Of course," Elizabeth replied.

"Lord Kirkheathe is not here to stop you," Rual agreed.

Elizabeth paused. Now that she knew why Raymond had treated them as she had, she did not fear his anger. "I see no harm talking to the woman at the gatehouse, and perhaps providing her with a little aid. She must be desperate to seek me out after the way my husband treated them. Please take a count of the ale casks for me while I am with her."

As she hurried out of the building toward the imposing gatehouse, she hoped Rual could count.

She spotted the distraught and shivering woman pacing uneasily near the bossed gates.

"Oh, my lady," the woman wailed, sinking to her knees as Elizabeth hurried to her.

"What is it?" Elizabeth cried, helping her to her feet. "Are you ill?"

"No, I'm not ill, my lady."

"Thank God. But what is the matter? Where is Erick?"

"With his father in a ruined hut not far from here. I...I came because we are starving, my lady. My husband doesn't know I've come here. He thinks I'm foraging for food in the wood, but we can't live off what I can find. My milk is nearly gone and I...I—"

She began to sob.

Whatever Raymond thought and despite her promise to consult with him about charitable gifts, Elizabeth could not send her away empty-handed.

"Say no more for now," Elizabeth urged softly. "Come with me to the kitchen. I will get you some food."

"Oh, thank you, my lady!"

"What is your name?"

She wiped her eyes. "Hildagard, my lady."

Elizabeth gave her a warm smile. "I will get you some food."

Anxiously twisting the cuff of the sleeve of her simple homespun gown, she said, "Your husband will not approve."

"He may not be pleased, but he will not be angry once I explain," Elizabeth assured her.

"I...that is, I've hurt my arm. I don't think I can carry anything much."

"Then I will come with you to help you. I would love to see Erick again."

"Will you...will you bring soldiers?"

Elizabeth regarded her steadily. "Should I not?"

"Your lord may not like it. I would hate to cause you trouble."

"As I said, Lord Kirkheathe will understand when I explain. At present he is not home."

"But he might hear of it when he returns, and be angry with you again."

Elizabeth smiled. "I will risk it to see your fine boy again. Besides, this way, we can take twice as much. Now come with me."

Elizabeth escorted the still obviously fearful Hildagard to the kitchen. Once there, Elizabeth briskly ordered one of the spit boys to fetch two baskets—a large one for her to carry, and a smaller one for Hildagard—a scullery maid to find squares of linen to line them, and Lud to get some bread and meat.

If they thought her orders odd, or remembered the stranger's face, they said nothing, but quietly obeyed.

"Sit a moment while I fetch my cloak and something warmer for you, Hildagard," Elizabeth said. "I won't be long."

She hurried off toward her bedchamber, leaving Hildagard sitting in the kitchen.

While she waited for her patroness to return, Hildagard continued to twist the worn end of her sleeve with her thin, nervous fingers.

Chapter Twelve

After returning to Hildagard and leaving the kitchen with her, Elizabeth pulled the woman into the small, shadowed area between the kitchen and the well. Their baskets jostled together, and Elizabeth set hers upon the ground. Then she took off her hooded cloak.

"My lady?" Hildagard asked as she pulled the shawl Elizabeth had brought around her. Hildagard had demurred, but Elizabeth had insisted she take it and keep it. She told the shivering woman it was old and she had no more use for it, and that was true. Raymond was proving to be far more generous than she had ever dreamed possible, and had bought her a warm wool shawl so soft, she was always tempted to rub it against her cheek the whole time she wore it.

"We need a little trickery, Hildagard," Elizabeth explained while turning her garment inside out, so that the plain woolen lining, the same brown color as Rual's cloak, was on the outside. "With my cloak this way and my hood pulled over my head, I could be Rual. She is busy counting the ale barrels, and we should be out of the village before she's finished."

Hildagard looked far from convinced of the effect of the disguise.

"Well, it should be enough to fool the guards, if you talk to me as if I am Rual. After all, they won't be expecting me to leave."

"Are you certain of this, my lady?"

"Perfectly. We must get this food to your family, and I want to see your fine son." She smiled at her companion. "I also have some things I want to ask you, about when you were with child."

Hildagard's eyes widened, as did Elizabeth's smile. "Yes, I think so," she said in answer to Hildagard's unspoken question.

"Oh, my lady!" Hildagard smiled. "I will be happy to answer any questions I can. My mother was a midwife."

"Truly? Are you?"

Hildagard shook her head. "Sadly, I am not. My mother died a few years ago, before I had learned all she had to teach. I remember much she told me, but not enough to call myself a midwife." Doubt appeared on her wan features. "Perhaps you should stay here."

"I feel fine," Elizabeth protested. "Indeed, I haven't felt so well in many years. And I think the walk will do me good. If your family is in the ruined hut near the river, it is not far.''

''You know of the place?''

''Indeed, I do,'' Elizabeth said, feeling a blush steal over her face as she remembered the day she had first seen it. ''I'm surprised we didn't find you there.''

''We...we haven't been there long.''

''No?'' Elizabeth asked lightly. ''Well, I am very glad you are there now, so that I can help you. Now come, and as we near the gate, you must speak to me as if I am Rual. Lady Kirkheathe gave you food and told me to come with you. Do you understand?''

Hildagard nodded.

''Very well, then, let us see if we can't sneak past the guards.''

Picking up her basket of food, and with her head bent, Elizabeth started toward the gate. Hildagard hurried along beside her.

When they neared the guards, Elizabeth began to fear Hildagard was too timid to do as she suggested. She slowed her brisk pace and loudly cleared her throat.

Hildagard started like a deer in a meadow, then said, ''It is very good of your lady to be so generous to us.'' Her voice was strained, but no more than it had been when she arrived, and Elizabeth hoped the guards would not think her obvious nervousness caused by anything overly suspicious.

''I'm sure you'll be back in time to serve the evening meal," Hildagard continued. "It must be very pleasant work here."

Her eyes on the ground, Elizabeth watched the toes of the guards' boots as they passed by them.

"Your lord is a very frightening man, though. I would be trembling all the while I was in the hall, I'm sure."

With Hildagard continuing to make such observations, they went on through the village without attracting any undue notice because it was crowded, this being market day. The villagers were either too busy buying or selling to pay much heed to two women hurrying along with baskets on their arms as if they were shopping, too.

Once out of sight of the houses, Elizabeth threw off her hood and grinned. "There now, that wasn't so difficult, was it? In fact, it was so easy, I may have to speak to my husband about his guards' vigilance when he returns."

"I don't want to get anyone in trouble," Hildagard murmured.

"I will not be talking about today particularly, you can be sure of that," Elizabeth said as they left the main road to follow the path Hildagard pointed out, which went in the direction of the river. "I will speak in generalities. I wouldn't want to get any of the guards in trouble, either."

"You wished to speak of childbearing, my lady?"

"Yes. I thought women were always sick when they were with child."

Hildagard grinned. "Some are, and some are not. It depends upon the woman."

"Good, because as I said, I have never felt better in my life. Nevertheless, I am over a se'ennight beyond my usual time, and I have never been this late before."

"Are your breasts tender, my lady?"

"They have been since before my husband left, but I thought perhaps it was because...well, I hoped, but..."

Hildagard smiled knowingly. "If they are still tender and he has been gone some days, and you have not yet come into your woman's time, I think it might very well be the other."

"I do hope so, Hildagard!"

"I think you will be a fine mother, my lady."

"I love children."

"Even when they're naughty?"

"Considering I was always told I was a bad girl, perhaps especially so."

Hildagard gave her an incredulous look.

"I assure you, it's true," Elizabeth confirmed. "Full of original sin, homely and hopeless."

"Homely?"

"Ugly as the devil was the Reverend Mother's favorite description of me," Elizabeth explained.

"Was she blind?"

Elizabeth had to laugh at Hildagard's question. "No, she could see very well. Indeed, some of the girls thought she must have eyes in the back of her head, too. Nothing much ever got past her.''

Except me, Elizabeth finished inwardly, and with the satisfaction that knowledge always gave her.

''Well, she must have been a very hardhearted woman to say something so cruel.''

''Yes, she was.''

''You have not had as easy a life as I thought.''

''My life has been easier than some, I allow, but it was very hard at the convent. Very hard.'' Elizabeth sighed, then smiled again. ''But I am very happy now, and if I have a child, all my prayers will be answered.''

Hildagard's footsteps slowed and Elizabeth watched her face, seeing the struggle there.

Elizabeth smiled sympathetically. ''Have no fear, Hildagard,'' she said softly. ''I know what—or who—probably waits at the hut, and it isn't your husband and son. Are they kept in Montross's castle? Once you deliver me there, are they to be freed?''

Hildagard stared at her with disbelief, then her face seemed to crumple and she began to weep. ''He said...he said we would be free to go if I did this. Otherwise, he could accuse my husband of poaching and put him in his dungeon for a long time. Then what would become of Erick and me? Oh, my lady, I'm so sorry! You were so good to us and this is how I repay you.''

Elizabeth took hold of the woman's shaking shoulders. "Hildagard, where is your family now?"

"In the hut. With him."

"Thanks be to God for that!" Elizabeth said softly.

Hildagard took her hands from her face and looked at her.

"If they are there," Elizabeth explained, "it should be easy for you to get away. I was much more concerned that he had them in his castle. I'm not sure what we would have done then." She wiped the tears from Hildagard's cheek. "You must stop crying, or he will know that I suspected a trap."

"How...how did you know?"

"My husband once asked if I am a seer, but it is nothing so special as that," Elizabeth replied. "It was obvious to me that there was more to your plea than hunger because you were so very desperate, even when you saw that I was going to help. Since you were alone, I reasoned somebody was forcing you, and keeping your family as hostage to ensure that you did what they wanted. My husband has one enemy that I know of close at hand, and one who seems the kind to use a woman against her husband."

"My lady," Hildagard said, "if you are not a seer, you are very clever."

"At the convent, the only thing I had to study was the women there. After thirteen years, I should hope I would have learned something about people.''

Hildagard's eyes once more filled with tears. ''Oh, my lady, please know that if he did not hold my son, no power on earth would make me betray you.''

Elizabeth smiled with both sorrow and understanding. ''I can believe that, Hildagard. Nevertheless, once you are safely away, I think we will not meet again, so I will say my farewell now. Goodbye, Hildagard.''

Hildagard grabbed her hand and pressed a grateful kiss upon it. ''Bless you, my lady.''

''Come along, Hildagard.''

''Yes, my lady.''

Elizabeth marched purposefully toward the hut. She spotted the peddler's wagon and horse nearby. Meanwhile, Hildagard hurried along behind, wiping the remains of the tears from her cheeks.

When Elizabeth reached the hut, she went around what was left of the outer wall. Holding a slumbering Erick, the peddler sat in a corner. He had his terrified eyes on Sir Fane Montross, who held a drawn sword.

''Sir Fane!'' she cried in apparent surprise as she handed her basket to Hildagard, who had no trouble holding it. ''What are you doing?''

Montross quickly sheathed his sword. ''My lady, you came upon me so suddenly. I was showing this peddler my sword. He asked to see it.''

She could almost admire the facility with which Montross lied. "It looked as if you were threatening him," she remarked as Hildagard hurried to join her husband and son.

"God's wounds, no!" he protested.

"It is an interesting coincidence that we meet here in the woods," she said as Hildagard took Erick in her arms. "As you no doubt already know, Sir Fane, my husband does not approve of traveling tinkers or peddlers or entertainers. Fortunately, he is away in Chesney at present, so when Hildagard came to me for aid, I was glad to help her. But really," she continued, addressing them, "you must take these things and leave at once. If my husband discovers you have returned to his estate…" She let her words trail off significantly.

"Forgive us, my lady," the peddler said as he bobbed a bow. "We'll go. At once."

"And I think it would be wise if you never returned."

"No, my lady, not never," he eagerly agreed.

She watched as they hurried to the wagon. After putting the baskets in the cart, the man took Erick, who awoke and started to wail. He held him while his wife climbed up on the rough wooden seat. Then he handed her the baby, got beside her and urged his horse into a brisk trot down the narrow way.

"I fear my husband was very brusque with them before," she remarked to Montross. "I must confess

I'm surprised they had the audacity to come to me for aid.''

Montross regarded her with an approving smile. ''It is obvious that you are a kind and gentle lady. No doubt that is why.''

''Tell me, Sir Fane, why are you on my husband's land?''

''I was fowling and one of my birds came this way. I was looking for him.''

''All by yourself?''

''I saw no need to bring my entire party after one hawk.''

''I see.''

''Just as you obviously saw no need to bring a troop of men on your errand, my lovely lady.''

While Elizabeth now knew there was some truth to his compliment, it was all she could do to keep a smirk from her face. ''You flatter me, sir.''

''My lady,'' he said, looking at her with what she supposed he meant for grave intensity, though it was a pale imitation of her husband's, ''I must express my gratitude for your kind and welcoming behavior toward me at your husband's castle. You know why I could not stay, but I appreciate your treatment of me nonetheless.''

''You were a guest in my home. Naturally I had to make you welcome.''

''Oh, but there was more to your kindness than mere duty,'' he said quietly, moving a little closer.

''No, there was not,'' she said bluntly. ''And I

would advise you, Sir Fane, to keep your distance.''
She frowned. "Tell me, do I look stupid as well as
pretty? I must, if you think me so foolish as to come
here without protection and not to realize that something was very amiss when Hildagard arrived as she
did.''

The man scowled. "I had no idea those paupers
were here, and obviously I had no plan to try to
harm you, or I would not have sheathed my sword.''

"You were certainly planning on unsheathing
something, unless I miss my guess. You were going
to try to seduce me, weren't you? Perhaps not today—even you might doubt that you have sufficient
prowess for such a swift conquest. But you were
hoping to begin. What were you going to say? That
I am too good for my husband? That I am beautiful,
and such beauty is wasted on him?

"Or were you going to play the valiant protector,
filling my ears with tales of my husband's evil, suggesting that he must be wicked to have driven your
sister to try to kill him, and that she had been cruelly
used while she was his wife?''

"I intended to do nothing of the sort," Montross
replied between clenched teeth. "I was merely riding through this wood looking for my peregrine. I
came upon the peddler by chance.''

"If that is so, clearly I was seriously mistaken,"
she replied evenly.

"It is the truth.''

She cocked her head to regard him as she might

an interesting bug. "Then you have my apologies for thinking you found me attractive."

"I do find you attractive, my lady. Very. And I also believe it is as you say. You are wasted on Kirkheathe."

"I would be so much happier with you?"

"I would do all in my power to make you happy."

She smiled.

He smiled.

"Ah, Sir Fane, I will give you this, you are persistent."

"Perhaps because I fell in love with you the moment I saw you."

"You did?"

"I did. You are the most beautiful woman I have ever seen."

"And you are the most outrageous liar I have ever met, and you must also believe me to be a vain and stupid woman to be won over by such lies," Elizabeth retorted, all vestige of feigned pleasure gone in the blink of an eye. "The moment I saw you, I knew you loathed and envied my husband. You and he are enemies, and I was never more sure that my husband's enmity had just cause than I am now. Only a base coward goes at a man through his wife. Now if I were you, I would get on my horse and ride back to my estate as fast as I could, before I take fright and call upon my husband's archers to protect me. Twenty of his finest are in the trees surrounding us. They came on ahead while I delayed a little. I have but to raise my hand and you will have an arrow in your chest.''

Montross's jaw dropped, revealing that while he might be fair of face, his teeth were rotting. "You wouldn't dare!"

"Would you care to put my resolution to the test?"

He glared at her. "I don't believe you."

"You should. My husband had no need to take his archers to Chesney, had he? Therefore, he did not."

Montross glared at her an instant longer, then turned tail and ran to his horse.

"No, my fine vain enemy," she murmured as she watched him flee. "I am not a fool."

She smiled with satisfaction and then called for the men to get down from the trees.

Because it was market day, Raymond had no choice but to walk his horse through the crowded streets of the village. Impatient, he had ridden on ahead of his men. Tempted though he was to continue at a gallop, if he tried to do so in the crowded streets, he might injure or even kill someone.

Besides, he told himself, if there were anything seriously amiss at Donhallow, Barden would have sent word. He had encountered no such bearer of tidings from home.

Now, as he encountered the surprised glances of

his people, he wondered if he had been foolish to return as he had. He had risked the earl's displeasure leaving Chesney without a word and apparently for nothing.

Nevertheless, he would not rest easy until he saw Elizabeth alive and well.

Finally, he was at the gates and through, and back in his own courtyard.

There was a troop of archers there, milling about as if they had just returned from a practice. However, he could see no carts bearing straw and targets, and the arrows in their sheaths…the arrows in the sheaths were the best they had, not the blunter ones kept for practice.

A cold finger of fear slid along Raymond's spine as he strode toward the serjeant-at-arms, who quickly came to meet him.

"My lord," Hale said, bowing. He didn't look particularly tense, but then why did the men have the expensive arrows? "We did not expect you back so soon. Where is your escort?"

"They follow."

"If we'd known, she would have waited for you, no doubt."

Raymond did not need to ask who. "To do what?"

"To go with that peddler's wife."

Relief gave way to anger that, after all he had said, she would disobey his wishes and put herself

at risk, as well as waste food they could ill afford
to spare.

Hale blanched. "Forgive me if I have done wrong
to do as she bid me, my lord, but she's your wife.
I was bound to obey her."

"Did Barden not protest?"

"He tried, my lord, but—"

He didn't get to complete his answer, for Raymond was already striding toward the hall.

Chapter Thirteen

Raymond didn't need to hear more. Elizabeth had to be made to understand that she was simply not as free as she might like to believe. He had his reasons for what he commanded, and if any harm had come to her—!

Before he reached the hall, Elizabeth came running out, happiness lighting her pretty face. "My lord, you are back so soon! What a delightful—" She halted in confusion. "What is it? What's the matter? What happened in Chesney?"

He would not voice his anger in public. "To the solar," he snapped, marching past her.

He heard her swift footfalls hurrying after him and was grimly glad. Once in the solar, he whirled around and faced her.

"My lord, whatever is the matter?" she repeated as she came inside and closed the door. "Please tell me. You're frightening me."

"Now you know something of my feeling when Hale told me what you did today."

"You were frightened?"

He nodded, realized that beneath his anger, that was what had truly filled him as he listened to Hale. "Montross is a dangerous man, Elizabeth."

"I know and you told me I must not go out of Donhallow unprotected. That is why I took the archers with me, so I would be safe when he met me."

Dumbfounded, Raymond stared at her. Hale had not mentioned this.

"Yes, my lord, Montross was there, as I thought he would be," she replied calmly. "As I suspected, it was a trap. He sent Hildagard, the peddler's wife, to beg my help and waited for me to come back with her."

Raymond could scarcely draw breath.

"Fortunately, I guessed aright about how he thought to have his revenge on you, and he had none of his men with him."

"How?"

"It was his intention to try to seduce me."

Raymond had to sit down.

"Hildagard was terrified when she came here," Elizabeth explained. "Far more terrified than she should have been, even though you had been harsh. After all, *I* had been most sympathetic, and since she didn't venture past the gate, she should have been at least a little relieved to see me and to hear

I was going to help her. Instead, she was more upset than ever.

"So I thought it must be a ruse to get me outside the castle. Who would do that, and why? The only person I could think of was your enemy, my lord.

"As for the why, I thought he might try to kill me, or seduce me. Given what I had seen of him, I suspected the latter. He is vain enough to believe that he could seduce any woman, and coward enough to try to strike at you through your wife."

God's wounds, she guessed all that? She was by far the shrewdest woman he had ever met.

"It is not so surprising that I surmised so much, my lord," she said with a gentle smile. "There were always girls who tried to hurt those they disliked by turning their friends against them. He is no different."

"Whatever the reason," Raymond growled, impressed and also dismayed by this glimpse into the cloistered life, "you should not have gone."

"I had to, my lord, or he would most certainly have harmed the peddler's family. You know that as well as I, if not better."

His wife would put her life at risk because of some peddler and his family? "Elizabeth," he chided.

"You think me reckless, but I sent your best archers, so I was sure I would be quite safe. My greatest fear was that Hildagard would wonder why the guards apparently didn't recognize their lord's wife, in spite of my attempt at a disguise.''

Raymond rose and went to her, taking her hands in his and gazing into her bright, fearless eyes. ''He could have killed you nonetheless.''

''He would have had to draw his sword to do that, my lord. I kept my distance, so he would have to come to me, leaving plenty of time for one of your fine archers to hit him. That is why I took the archers and not foot soldiers.''

Raymond gazed at her in wonderment.

''The worst was not knowing where he had Hildagard's husband and child. If he meant to kill me, they could have been in his castle. Fortunately, I hadn't underestimated his vanity, and he had them with him, to maintain the deception that our meeting was by chance. He claimed he was on your land searching for an errant hawk.

''All turned out well, Raymond. The peddler's family got away, and Montross understands he has no hope of coming between you and me. I think that is worth whatever risk I took.''

He pulled her into his arms and embraced her tightly. ''I do not. If he had killed you...'' He could not finish, for he could not begin to find the words to say how that would hurt him.

''But he didn't,'' Elizabeth murmured, snuggling against him. ''Oh, my lord, I am glad you have come home!'' she sighed. ''I missed you so.''

''Raymond.''

She drew back a little. "My lord?"

"I would have you call me by my name."

Her smile was glorious. "Very well, my...Raymond."

"My Raymond sounds even better."

She laughed, and so did he.

"My Raymond, there is something more to tell you."

He raised a brow, wondering what else she had done in his absence. Perhaps he had relaxed too soon.

"I believe I am with child."

Dread disappeared as a happiness such as he had never known swept over him. Their child. She was carrying their child.

He swept her off her feet and turned in a wild, dizzying circle.

"Put me down, or I fear I shall be ill."

He did at once.

She looked at him, and smiled. "No need to look so stricken. I am not sick. I have not had a day's illness yet."

"Not at all?"

"I was concerned about that, too, but Hildagard's mother was a midwife and she said not every woman feels ill when she is with child. I am late more than a se'ennight, and I have never been late in my life. Also, there are other symptoms."

"Such as?"

With a wry smile, she raised his hand and put it

on her breast. "A light touch there, if you please, my lord, and no more."

"Oh."

"Oh, and since you are now so serious, I will ask you why you have come home so soon from Chesney. I thought you would be some days yet. Or dare I hope it was because you missed me?"

The heat of embarrassment traveled up his face, something he had not experienced in a long time. "That, too."

She frowned. "Too? That is not the main reason you returned?"

"There is that pout again," he noted, tugging her to him and kissing her in a way that should show he had missed her very much indeed.

She relaxed into his embrace and he marveled that every kiss seemed even more exciting than the last.

Then, too soon, she pulled away and smiled, the warmth in her eyes touching him. "I missed that, too." She frowned again. "What was the real reason you came back so soon?"

Taking her hand, he led her to the chair, sat and gently pulled her onto his lap. "Fane Montross was not in Chesney," he said, wrapping his arms loosely about her.

"And he should have been?"

Raymond nodded. "He is closer to the earl than I."

"So you came home because you feared what he might do?"

"With good cause."

"Was the earl surprised by your sudden departure? If he and Montross are friendly…"

"I did not speak to the earl."

"Not at all?"

Raymond shook his head.

"Yet you were so pleased to be asked to his council."

"I was more worried about you."

"Really?"

"Really. And I was right."

"I don't know what you mean," she said with feigned innocence.

"Yes, you do."

She smiled a moment, then genuine concern darkened her face. "I hope the earl does not take offense. He invited you to his castle, and then you leave without speaking to him."

When Raymond believed Montross was up to something, he had dismissed that worry. Now that all was well—although it might have turned out otherwise—he had to acknowledge that the earl might very well take great offense. Nevertheless, he would not burden his wife with that, so he shrugged.

Her face brightened. "I know what we can do to mend any breach there may be with the earl.

"We shall invite him to visit us here. We can tell him you were concerned about my health, which is no lie. Of course, he may think you meant my being with child when he arrives. Still, we have no need to go into details. Then, when he comes, we will ensure he understands that you were very honored by the invitation and regret that you left in such unseemly haste.''

He kissed her cheek. ''You are a clever woman,'' he said. ''But he goes to London in a fortnight.''

''Then afterward. We could invite him to come when he returns.''

Raymond decided he had no choice but to tell her why they could not do as she suggested. ''We cannot afford it.''

Her brow wrinkled. ''Is he so very expensive a guest? How many men will he bring? Surely not more than fifty.''

''Five or fifty makes no difference,'' Raymond replied. ''We cannot afford to entertain in any style.''

''But you are rich!''

He shook his head.

''My uncle said—''

''He was wrong.''

''Wrong?''

''Wrong. I am nearly penniless.''

''Yet this castle—''

''Is expensive to man and maintain, and the income from my tenants is barely sufficient to cover food and the taxes.'' He reached up to touch her face. ''Donhallow is ancient, and needs many repairs. If not, it will crumble around us.''

He saw understanding growing in her eyes. ''And

the bridges and roads on the estate, too?'' she queried.

''Yes. I spent the last of my ready money preparing for your arrival, to impress your uncle. That is why I insisted he leave the day after we married. I didn't want to spend any more.''

''You should have asked him for more money for my dowry.''

''I didn't want to lose you.''

She blinked. ''What did you say?''

''I did not want to lose you.''

Her face flushed, the roses blooming in her cheeks making her more lovely than ever. ''Even then?''

''Even then.''

She gave him a long, slow kiss that made him regret not making this confession sooner.

Then she drew back and fixed him with a chastising look. ''You certainly gave no sign of that, my lord.''

He grinned.

''I think you, sir, could have made a fortune as a charlatan.''

''The fortune would be welcome, at any rate,'' he observed.

''How much *was* my dowry?''

''Five hundred marks.''

She gasped. ''But that is a huge sum!''

''What is left is necessary for repairs.''

''What is left?'' she repeated questioningly.

''I have already spent all I could spare.''

She wiggled off his lap and stared at him, arms akimbo. "Spent? On what?"

Raymond discovered he could still feel sheepish, too. "On presents for my wife."

She put her hand to her chest. "On me?" she whispered.

"On your new clothes, and more in Chesney."

"This is terrible!"

"That is not the reaction I had counted on."

"But my...Raymond! You shouldn't have, and if I had known—"

"It is too late to speculate on that now."

"But surely there must be some left to provide a few special dishes..."

He shook his head again.

"Not even a little?"

"A very little."

He watched as she started to pace briskly, and realized her mind was working with even more speed. "How long before he could come here, do you think?"

"Five months at the earliest. He goes to France after London."

"Wonderful! Five months should be long enough for us to save the necessary funds."

"Elizabeth, he never travels with less than thirty men, plus his wife and servants."

She paused and fixed her keen gaze on him. "How many people in total, do you think?"

"Forty at the least."

"Well, five months takes us through the spring and into summer," she began thoughtfully. As she continued, she grew eager. "I have seen the stores, and the linen is quite good enough, if plain. And we certainly have the room. A little good planning, some careful management of our resources...yes, five months and we could do it!"

A few moments ago, when she had first proposed the visit, he had been absolutely certain it was foolhardy even to think of it.

But now, as his pretty wife stood before him, her eyes shining, her whole body alight with suppressed excitement and happiness, he could believe that not only could they find the money to cover the cost, but that the earl was in for the most pleasant and comfortable visit of his life.

Five months later, Elizabeth gasped and shoved her pricked finger into her mouth.

Raymond stopped strumming the harp and glanced at her worriedly. Sprawled on the floor beside him, Cadmus opened one eye.

She had been delighted by his present, but after he had corrected her several times, she had persuaded him to play and discovered that he was a far better musician than she. In the days that followed, they learned to make music together. She would sing, and he would accompany her.

"It's nothing," she assured him as she checked to make sure no blood from her finger had fallen on the napkin she was embroidering. "But that is the fourth time this afternoon I have done this. I tell you, Raymond, it would have been much better if the Reverend Mother had made me sew as much as she had me scrub the floors. I would undoubtedly be much better at it."

"You do well enough," he said, picking up the harp again. "Sing that song I like, about the spring."

Elizabeth gladly set aside the detestable sewing and placed her hands in her lap below her rounded belly. She began to sing, and as she did, she watched him play. She liked to do that, especially when he didn't know she was watching. While he played, it was as if all the cares of his life melted away.

Just as they did when they were in bed together.

She felt a rolling motion inside her. "Oh, Raymond, quick! The baby is moving again," she cried happily.

Her husband set down his instrument and rushed to her side, placing his hand on her stomach.

His smile delighted her as much as the baby's movement. "I think the babe is going to be very strong," she noted.

She saw Raymond's face cloud. "I am very strong, too," she reminded him. "Didn't the village midwife say so? Please don't worry, Raymond. My mother was up and about the day after I was born, or so they say. Indeed, my aunts seemed to think she was impertinent to do so."

Raymond straightened. "Nevertheless, I've sent for a midwife from Chesney."

"But Raymond, that will cost so much!" Elizabeth's brow lowered and her indignation was only partly feigned. "Here I have been trying so hard to save money for the earl's visit, and you do something silly like that."

Her husband knelt beside her low chair and looked deep into her eyes. "I insist."

"I think it's a waste."

"I will not lose you in childbirth."

It was on the tip of her tongue to remind him again that she was perfectly healthy, but when she gazed into his eyes, she could not. "Very well, my Raymond. We shall have the midwife—but more for your sake than for mine. Just as long as I don't have to have a physician and an apothecary and a priest all milling about, too. I daresay I will not be at my best."

"Not unless I think them necessary," he agreed.

Deciding it was time to change the subject, she asked, "Tell me, what did Aiken say this morning about the bridges? Are they nearly finished with the repairs?"

Raymond rose and went to put away the harp. "The important ones are. The rest should be before winter."

"Good." She watched him a moment, then thought there might be no better time to broach a subject she had already delayed mentioning. "We will have to invite Montross to the feast for the earl.''

Her husband glanced at her sharply.

"He is the earl's vassal, too.''

"He is my enemy.''

"And mine, too,'' she agreed. "Nevertheless, I think we should do the courteous thing—and the wise thing,'' she hastened to add before he could protest. "If you do, and he refuses to come, nobody can reproach you.''

"I don't want him here.''

"I know. Neither do I. But I don't think he'll accept anyway, so what harm inviting him? Then if the earl asks or comments, you can say you did, and he refused. Who looks the worse under those circumstances?''

"You do not know Montross as I do. He has gall.''

"Then let him come. Indeed, let him come and see you with the earl. It may be something he should witness for himself, to understand that you are not without some influence now, as well.''

He still looked doubtful.

"My lord,'' she said, using the term she instinctively did when she wanted to make her point strongly, "did you not tell me when you returned from Chesney that your marriage to me has given you connections to some of the most powerful barons in the land?''

"Yes. The DeLanyeas of Wales, and DeGuerre.''

"Then why be afraid to invite Montross?"

"I am *not* afraid," he growled.

"He will say you are if you do not," she pointed out.

He blinked. "God's wounds," he said, regarding her with a mixture of pride and awe. "What a wise warrior I have wed."

She laughed softly. "There is but one warrior here, my lord, and it is not I."

"I disagree."

"I don't want to be a warrior. I would rather be a wife."

"You are the best wife a man could have," he assured her tenderly, drawing her to her feet and looking deep into her eyes. "A wife as fierce as any warrior, wise as one twice her age, and a worthy mother for my son."

"The babe may prove to be a daughter," she whispered, her breath coming fast as his eyes darkened with passion.

"Then a son after."

"I hope to bear you many sons and daughters, my Raymond."

"Whatever God wills, I will be content, for he has already given me a gift more rare than any gemstone and more precious than my lost voice."

She held him tight, loving him, needing him, basking in the warm glow of his tender, heartfelt words.

Then suddenly, from outside in the courtyard, she

heard a noise. A horrible, terrible, familiar sound that made her break from his arms and dash to the window.

"What is it?" Raymond demanded as he followed her. "Who has come?"

Chapter Fourteen

"Is it Montross?" Raymond demanded. "The earl too soon?"

Cadmus barked as if also asking what was the matter.

Meanwhile, Elizabeth continued to stare at the person who had ridden into the courtyard, a small mounted guard behind her. "It's the Reverend Mother."

"From the Convent of the Blessed Sacrament?"

"Yes." Elizabeth gripped the edge of the window and watched as the stout woman got off her white horse. "Why has she come? What does she want?"

"Sit down," Raymond said, taking her arm. "You look ill."

Elizabeth felt ill, sick with the memories of that hated voice and even more hated face, as well as the hand that struck the blows. "It must have been my letter to the bishop."

Raymond picked her up and carried her toward the bed. "You must lie down," he ordered gently.

She leaned her head against him, feeling protected and cherished.

"I will speak with her," he said as he laid her on the bed.

Elizabeth half rose, her arms behind her for support. "No," she said firmly. She swung her legs over the side and prepared to stand. "I am not a frightened, hungry child any more. I am the wife of Lord Kirkheathe."

"Beloved wife," he amended as he helped her to her feet. "Yet I think she will want to speak to me as well."

Elizabeth looked up at his grimly resolute face. "Why?"

"Because I added to your letter."

"You added to it?"

He inclined his head. "I wrote that I believed every word you said and the woman should be removed from her high office."

"You did?"

One more nod. "Stay here and rest," he ordered. "Let me deal with her."

"And have her think me a coward, afraid to face her? After all I have said to you about Montross? Oh, no, Raymond, I cannot."

"You are sure you are well enough?"

"I have felt better in my time, but I am not going to plead an indisposition." Then she smiled and put her hand in his. "Besides, I want her to see me with my husband. She always claimed I would come to a bad end, and I want her to discover how wrong she was."

"Just as I would like to meet the woman who thought she could break your spirit."

Together they left their chamber, followed by Cadmus.

As they went down the steps and entered the hall, Elizabeth realized all trace of her kind and tenderly affectionate husband had disappeared from the man beside her, as if they had been transported back in time to the day of their first meeting.

She had nearly forgotten how cold and imposing Raymond had been that day, and how much he had frightened her.

The Reverend Mother stood near the hearth, and she turned toward them when she heard them approach. The woman seemed to have aged in the past months. There were new lines of worry about her mouth and eyes.

Yet as she watched them draw near, her brow wrinkled with consternation, an expression Elizabeth remembered well. And although she was fond of dogs, including her own great brute who had attacked Elizabeth two years ago, she eyed Cadmus warily.

He began to growl, a low rumble of menace emanating from the back of his throat, and that seemed to disturb the woman even more.

Elizabeth almost felt like patting him on the head as he settled on his haunches beside Raymond when they halted.

"Mother," Elizabeth said, giving a little bow to her old nemesis. "This is my husband, Lord Kirkheathe. My lord, this is the Reverend Mother Superior of the Convent of the Blessed Sacrament."

Raymond didn't say a word.

The Reverend Mother looked taken aback, but only for a moment before she addressed Elizabeth with her customary arrogance. "Elizabeth, I have come—"

"Lady Kirkheathe," Raymond growled, his voice even lower and more rough than usual.

The Reverend Mother went a little white. "Lady Kirkheathe," she began again, not quite so arrogantly. "I have come to demand that you retract those things you said in your infamous letter to the bishop."

Raymond crossed his arms.

The Reverend Mother took a step back.

"Won't you please sit down?" Elizabeth asked with cool politeness. "I do not like to stay on my feet overmuch in my condition."

It was almost painfully obvious that the Reverend Mother had not noticed—or taken the trouble to notice—that Elizabeth was with child.

Elizabeth took a seat in one of the chairs, and the Reverend Mother sat opposite. Raymond came to stand behind Elizabeth and she had no doubt he was glaring at the woman as only he could glare, for the Reverend Mother looked more discomforted than Elizabeth would have believed possible. "You wish to discuss the letter I wrote to somebody else?" she asked.

"The bishop told me what you said and—"

"Did he? I must say I'm surprised, considering it was very unflattering. I always assumed the bishop was a kind man, but apparently I was quite mistaken."

The Reverend Mother's thin lips became even thinner. "He told me because he was removing me from the convent and sending me to Ireland!" She spat the last word as if it were a curse.

"You always said we were all little barbarians going straight to hell," Elizabeth remarked. "You should feel right at home."

"I want you to write him again and retract your hateful, dishonest remarks."

"You are speaking to my wife," Raymond said as he put his hands on Elizabeth's shoulders. She had to fight to keep still as he slowly, and gently, kneaded her shoulders.

This was nearly as bad—or good—as having him caress her intimately in front of the woman.

The Reverend Mother looked as if she could scarcely believe her eyes, which probably wasn't far from the truth. "You...you owe it to me," she stammered, the last vestige of arrogant domination slipping away. "I took you in when nobody else wanted you."

Elizabeth reached up and covered her husband's right hand with hers in a gesture of undeniable alliance. "You had to. It was your duty and your obligation at the convent. My uncle paid you, too. In fact, he paid you very well."

"Eliz…" the Reverend Mother began. She glanced up at Raymond and amended her address. "Lady Kirkheathe, I did my duty by you and if you feel hard done by, perhaps you should look to your family, who left you in my charge."

"That did not give you license to starve and beat us."

Raymond came around the chair. "I know how you mistreated those girls," he said, and his tone was enough to make even Elizabeth shiver.

The Reverend Mother's eyes darted from one to the other. Her face red, she rose swiftly. "You know only what she has told you."

"I have seen the scars."

"She stole things."

"Food because you starved her and the others."

"That's a lie."

Raymond crossed the distance between them in an instant, and for a moment, Elizabeth feared he meant to grab the Reverend Mother and throttle her. Instead, he halted inches from her. "You would dare to call my wife a liar?"

When the Reverend Mother stared speechlessly,

he said, "I added my confirmation in that letter. Would you also presume to upbraid me?"

Elizabeth felt a horrified fascination as tears began to ooze out of the Reverend Mother's small black eyes and run down her plump red cheeks. "She has cost me my place," she sniveled.

"No," Elizabeth declared. "If there is fault here, look to yourself, and yourself alone."

Desperation in her eyes, the Reverend Mother wrung her hands as she looked past Raymond to Elizabeth. "I am too old to go to that awful place!" she spluttered. "I will die."

Raymond stepped back and out of the way as Elizabeth came toward her. She stared at the woman with unflinching scorn. "How many girls died because we were cold and not properly fed? Your dog ate more meat than we did."

"I did my duty!"

"No, you did not. You took our relatives' money and spent it on food and wine for you and your chosen few. Do you think we didn't know? Do you think the nuns who were not your favorites didn't know? That we all couldn't smell the food and that our stomachs didn't growl because of it?"

"It was hard work taking care of you all."

"Hard work ordering us about, you mean. We were supposed to be learning useful skills and to be sure, we did—scouring pots, washing linen, scrubbing those detestable floors. You treated us as ignorant slaves, and I will never forget it."

"I did my best."

"You did your worst. You are not welcome here. Good day, Mother."

In desperation, the Reverend Mother turned to Raymond. He raised his brow quizzically, and that was enough to send her back to Elizabeth. "Have you no mercy, no pity?" she pleaded.

Elizabeth nodded, and softly answered, "Oh, yes. I pity the Irish."

The Reverend Mother's mouth worked like a fish out of water for a moment, then she turned and all but ran from the hall.

Elizabeth sank back into the chair.

"Are you all right?" Raymond asked.

"I feel as if I have bearded a lion." She smiled up at him standing beside her. "Thank you for helping me."

"There is no need to thank me," he replied with a proud and loving smile. "You had her beaten long ago."

A week later, Raymond found Aiken waiting for him in the stable when he returned from leading a patrol of the perimeter of his estate. The man smiled, but his fidgeting feet told Raymond that something was troubling him.

He hoped Aiken wasn't going to ask for more money for repairs. They were stretched to the limit as it was.

"My lord," Aiken began after Raymond had dismounted and turned Castor over to one of the grooms to be brushed and bedded down. "Yes?"

"I, um, I need to speak with you."

"So I assumed."

"Outside, if you please, my lord," Aiken said, nodding at the door.

Cadmus lumbering beside them, Raymond went with him, and Aiken led him to the chapel, empty at this hour of the day save for the lingering scent of incense. "Well?" Raymond asked as Aiken looked about cautiously and Cadmus flopped down at his feet.

"Well, my lord, it's like this," Aiken began nervously. "I, um, I wanted a little sport the other night, and since the women in the village all gossip like fishwives, I decided to go farther afield, if you follow me, my lord."

"I don't see what your sport has to do with me."

"Normally, nothing, my lord, of course," Aiken replied, giving another nervous glance at the closed door. "I mean, a man's allowed a little relaxation, and if it costs him, it costs him. But no obligations, neither, eh?"

"Did you bring me here to discuss the merits of patronizing a whore?" Raymond inquired. He would have been amused, except that Aiken was clearly upset.

"No! No, my lord," Aiken cried. He cleared his throat and began in a more businesslike manner. "I went to the village near Montross's castle. There's a particular place there, my lord. The girls are clean and the pander honest.''

"I know the place."

"Oh, yes, I forgot. Well, there's this one girl there, Nell. Very pretty and very...talented. Seems she's Fane Montross's favorite—or at least she was until a fortnight ago.''

"What does this have to do with me?''

"She was right upset and after she'd had plenty of ale, she told me why. Seems he's gone to London to meet the earl of Chesney.''

Raymond uttered a curse. He should have expected something like this. Of course Montross would try to get to the earl before he arrived here, to bend his ear with his malicious lies.

Raymond had feared love would weaken him. It had definitely distracted him. "She was certain?''

"Very. Right angry with him, she was.''

"I see. I appreciate your telling me this, Aiken.''

"My lord?''

"Yes?''

"There's more.''

Raymond frowned.

"There was some pretty tough-looking fellows there, too, so I asked her who they were. Mercenaries, she said. Seems word's gone out that Montross is hiring.''

Again, Raymond muttered a curse. "How many?''

"About ten so far.''

"What reason does Montross give?"

"The usual—looking for men to protect his estate."

"From what?"

"From you."

"That base, disgusting liar," Raymond growled, his hands curling into fists. "I don't want his land."

Aiken backed away. "I know that, my lord. And so does anybody who knows you."

Raymond took a deep breath. "I hope the earl knows the truth," he said. "I do appreciate the warning, Aiken."

The man nodded. "Yes, well, I thought you ought to know before the earl comes," he said. "Now I'll see about them timbers for the footings."

Looking relieved, he quickly departed.

"*If* the earl comes," Raymond muttered as the chapel door banged closed. Who could say what poison Montross was spewing?

And after all Elizabeth's work...

He would not upset her unnecessarily, for it could well be that the earl would come as he had promised. As Charles had so eagerly pointed out, he was now allied to some powerful men and despite what Montross said, the earl might not want to risk offending them, even if he had no such concern for the couple who had invited him.

Still, she didn't need the dread that the earl might not come, or worse. It might cause her to lose sleep and become ill.

These days, as she grew larger with their unborn child, he was haunted by the dread that she would die in childbirth as his mother had. Not even her assurances that she felt perfectly well and healthy, or those of the village midwife, could take away his fear completely.

If she died, a part of him would die, too.

Although he had believed himself in love, Allicia's death had struck a blow to his pride and security more than his heart; Elizabeth's death would tear his heart in two.

Raymond left the chapel and, accompanied by Cadmus, strode across the courtyard and through the hall. He paused a moment to ask Rual, who was sprinkling herbs on the rushes on the floor, where his wife was.

"The solar, my lord," the always grim maidservant answered.

He nodded, then commanded Cadmus to stay before he continued on his way. Although she was getting used to him, Cadmus still made Elizabeth nervous.

When he reached the solar, he paused a moment on the threshold. Elizabeth was too absorbed in reading the parchment in her hand to hear him approach.

It looked like a letter.

Who would write to his wife?

Chapter Fifteen

Elizabeth looked up and gave him a beautiful smile. Holding onto the arm of the chair to steady herself, she rose. "All was well?"

"We saw nothing amiss," he answered truthfully.

"I have received a letter from Genevieve."

He came farther inside the solar. "Your cousin?"

"Yes, the woman you were supposed to marry. I wrote to her a little while ago."

"You said nothing to me."

A wrinkle of consternation appeared between her brows. "I should have asked permission?"

"No," he replied, and reminding himself that he didn't want to alarm her, he sat in the chair and planted a kiss on her cheek as he pulled her down onto his lap. "I am surprised you would want to correspond with her, considering the circumstances."

"Perhaps I wrote to thank her," Elizabeth said with a delightful hint of mischief in her eyes.

It was no wonder all thoughts of Montross and his machinations fled when he was with her, he reflected. "Is that really why?"

"Not precisely. I did assure her that I was happy, and I hoped she was, too."

"Is she?"

"Very much so, and she was most relieved to hear from me. Indeed, I think she was afraid I had been condemned to a horrible fate."

"Unflattering words, my love."

"Well, she never met you, did she?"

"No."

"Then she had only my uncle's description to go by, and he is not the man you want describing your person to anyone."

"So I shall blame him for your cousin's desperate act to avoid marrying me."

"But it has all turned out well, has it not?"

"Very well," he murmured, nuzzling her neck.

"That is not the only reason I wrote to her," Elizabeth continued with a sigh of pleasure. "I wanted to ask her about the earl's sister."

Raymond pulled back. "The earl's sister?"

"Yes," Elizabeth replied with an eager nod. "I thought the earl of Chesney's sister, Maude, arrived the day before I left Lady Katherine's, and Genevieve tells me I am right. She remembers her very well. She also remembers that Maude and her brother were quite close, and when she later died, he was very distraught."

"You aren't planning to speak of his sister to him?"

"Of course I shall! She was a sweet girl and very well liked by all at Lady Katherine's, including Lady Katherine herself—no small accomplishment, I assure you."

"Lady Katherine liked you, did she not?"

His wife reflected a moment. "Do you know, I believe she did. She was not given to demonstrations of feeling, rather like someone else I respect and admire," she noted, giving him a pointed yet affectionate look. "I recall that once, I told some girls to stop teasing a younger girl, and after that, there was always a sort of…I don't know…camaraderie in her eyes when she looked at me, as if we were friends."

"I think you bewitch people," he replied gravely. "You bewitched me."

"I didn't do anything of the kind," she retorted pertly. "I didn't even try to make you like me."

He grinned. "In that, you failed miserably."

She toyed with the neck of his tunic. "Did I?"

"Yes." He wondered if she was going to slip her hand inside.

Aroused by that thought, he had to shift her a bit for comfort.

"I am going to do my very best to make the earl like me, too."

His brow lowered with mock anger. "Are you trying to make me jealous again?" he growled.

"No," she replied with a laugh that showed just

how seriously she took his bogus accusation. "I am going to make the earl happy and comfortable, so that he thinks of us with favor."

"If there is anybody who can do that," Raymond replied, "it is you."

She did slip her hand inside his tunic, moving it slowly down to his collarbone. "Genevieve says she is very happily wed. I don't see how she can be."

"Why not?" he murmured as he closed his eyes and gave himself over to the pleasure of her touch.

"Because she doesn't have you for a husband. Poor dear. She has no idea of the opportunity she threw away."

"You could give Montross lessons in flattery."

She swiftly withdrew her hand. He opened his eyes and saw the worried look on her face, then silently cursed himself for bringing his enemy into the conversation.

"Has he sent a response to the invitation?" she asked.

"Not yet."

"I wonder if he won't bother replying and just come on the day of the feast."

Pleased that she wouldn't be caught completely off-guard by Montross's arrival if he did come with the earl, Raymond wrapped his arms around her swollen waist. "That would not surprise me. He may think to show us he is still a good friend of the earl's and does not fear me."

"Then we shall not be surprised, but prepared."

"You have done so much preparing, surely there is nothing that could go amiss," he said.

She gravely shook her head. "I'm sure there will be. I can only hope not too many things go wrong, and that the earl arrives tomorrow as he should."

"The weather is fine, the roads are good, and the bridges along the way repaired." He pulled her close and kissed her lightly. "You and your plans are very impressive."

She sighed as he continued to kiss her on her cheek, and then her neck. "My lord, it is nearly time for…"

"For…?"

"Something. I think…it must be…"

"Not important," he murmured as he moved his hands slowly up her arms and to her shoulders. One hand slipped around her back and the other fondled her breast, then encountered the rise of her belly.

He hesitated, thinking that what he so very much wanted to do might hurt her. "Shall I stop?"

"No, my darling," she sighed, arching back to expose her slender throat. "The midwife says not yet."

"Are you sure?"

"You are not the only one who would want to know, Raymond," she chided. "I asked her only yesterday."

Relieved and delighted, he chuckled softly.

And continued.

* * *

The next morning, Raymond stood on the steps of his great hall, his wife beside him. The sentry at the tower had sighted the earl's party approaching and they waited to welcome him.

He glanced down at Elizabeth, whose hands were clasped beneath her belly. She seemed the very picture of calm unless one knew her as he did. He could see the subtle tension in her shoulders.

He was glad she had already anticipated some skullduggery on Montross's part.

"Wait inside," he suggested, "where you can sit."

"No, I should be here beside you when he comes."

"You are with child."

"That doesn't mean I cannot stand."

"Are you certain?"

"If I do feel faint, I will not hesitate to tell you."

"Promise?"

She gave him a look. "I give you my solemn vow, my lord."

"Don't be angry."

"I'm not. I am nervous."

"You sound angry."

"If I do, it is because of your constant chatter!"

He gave her an incredulous look. He had never in his life been chastised for chattering, and certainly never after the injury to his throat.

"I'm sorry, Raymond," she said contritely.

"The midwife told me you might be moody."

"When did you last speak to her?"

"Yesterday, after…" He gave her a significant look.

"I told you she said it would be all right. Didn't you trust me?"

He felt the heat creeping into his face. "I had other things to ask."

"Such as?"

"I will not speak of them here," he muttered, surveying the courtyard and his soldiers arranged up there. Servants bustled to and fro finishing the final preparations, and those who had completed their tasks likewise waited, whispering among themselves so the sound of their murmuring made it like being near the sea.

"You might as well. We have nothing else to do until they arrive, and unless you start shouting, nobody will hear."

"It is a private matter."

"I am your wife." She gave him a sidelong glance. "Shall I pout? Will that encourage you to tell me?"

"Stick your lip out like that, and I am liable to kiss you."

"So kiss me."

"We are not alone."

"If you aren't going to kiss me, tell me what you spoke of to the midwife."

"You are not going to stop pestering me until I do, are you?"

"No."

He leaned down and whispered in her ear. "I wanted to know exactly how long before we had to stop making love."

She drew back, not a bit nonplussed. "I thought as much," she said with a triumphant little grin that made him want to sweep her up into his arms and carry her into their bedchamber at once, earl or no earl.

Then they heard the hoofbeats on the road approaching the gatehouse. Elizabeth slipped her hand into his, and he squeezed it.

His lovely wife had nothing to fear from the earl. She had worked and planned for this visit for five months, and done everything she could to see that the earl and his party would be comfortable at Donhallow. Not only that, she was pretty and spirited, two qualities that would win over the most recalcitrant man. After all, had she not completely captivated him?

If there was anything to fear, it was, as always, Fane Montross.

Once again Raymond silently cursed himself for not being more diligent. He had feared love would weaken him, and so it had—but not mortally so, he hoped. It all depended on what Montross told the earl, what his overlord believed, and what his overlord thought upon this visit.

Unfortunately, Raymond discovered that he had been right to worry about Montross's journey to

London when the earl rode though the gate, Montross at his side.

Elizabeth gasped, and he squeezed her hand again for reassurance, telling himself that even this need not signal trouble. After all, as Charles had said, he was now allied with some of the most powerful men in Britain, and the earl would know that. The scales had tipped, and it would take a great deal of effort on Montross's part to tip them back.

Still, the man was no doubt trying to do just that.

As the cortege drew to a halt, Elizabeth nodded at Montross and whispered, "Did you know Montross would arrive with the earl?"

"Not for certain."

She regarded him shrewdly. "You are not surprised, so you expected him to be with the earl."

"We will discuss this later."

"We certainly will, my lord," she murmured as they went down the steps to greet the earl of Chesney. He had dismounted, and his stocky body twisted and turned as he surveyed Donhallow Castle.

Raymond kept his gaze on Montross, who was staring at his wife as a wolf might eye a lamb alone.

He could kill Montross for that look alone.

"My lord," Raymond said as he drew near the earl and bowed.

The earl, his plump face scarred by smallpox, returned his smile. "Lord Kirkheathe."

"Allow me to present my wife, Elizabeth," Raymond continued proudly as she curtsied.

The earl addressed Montross, who stood nearby. "As you said, she is a beauty."

A shaft of possessive jealousy struck Raymond. How dare Montross describe his wife? And why had he sung her praises?

"Whatever beauty I have comes from my happiness, my lord," Elizabeth said to the earl, drawing his attention back to them. "And perhaps because I am with child. They say expecting a baby makes women glow."

The earl chuckled. "Aye, so they do. I can vouch for that. My own dear wife never looked better than when she was with child." He glanced back at his lady, a middle-aged woman of average height and no beauty whatsoever.

"Please, won't you and your party come into the hall? We have refreshments prepared," Elizabeth said. She turned toward Montross. "Sir Fane, too, of course."

She spoke with bland and faultless courtesy, yet her tone was very different from the friendlier one she had used when she addressed the earl.

He knew the distinction was not lost on the attentive earl, either, despite the jovial smile that never left the man's face.

The earl held his arm out to escort Elizabeth into the hall, while Raymond took the arm of Lady Chesney.

As he led the earl's wife into his hall, he was struck again by the results of Elizabeth's efforts and his companion's gasp of delight told him that he was not alone in his appreciation.

Elizabeth had found some larger tapestries stored in the far corner of a storage room. They had been dusty and full of tiny moth holes. After helping to beat out the dust—sneezing and laughing with the maidservants the whole while—she had set Rual to repairing them. They now graced the walls, while the plain furniture shone in the candlelight. Elizabeth had helped polish it with beeswax until he thought her arm would fall off. The rushes had been replaced that very morning, and sprinkled with sweet-smelling herbs. Not the most exotic or expensive, to be sure, but pleasant nonetheless.

The food they would have would also be not the most expensive or exotic, but ample. Elizabeth had assured him that the type of food was not so important as long as what they had was well-prepared. "Better to have plenty of good plain food than a scarcity of rich," she had decreed.

Despite his pride and pleasure in his wife and his hall, however, Raymond was also very aware that Montross was behind him.

And it wasn't long before he knew what Montross thought of his wife's efforts.

The moment they were all gathered round the hearth, Montross said, "Well, Raymond, I see the difference a wife can make to a wolf's den."

He didn't reply, and Elizabeth addressed the earl.

''My lord, I met your sister once, at Lady Katherine DuMonde's.''

A smile of delight spread over the earl's face. ''Did you indeed?''

''Yes, but briefly, I am sorry to say. My cousin knew her better, and speaks most highly of her.''

''She was very well-liked.''

''And an excellent dancer, Genevieve says. The best she ever saw.''

The earl's chest puffed out with pride, and his eyes seemed a little shinier. ''She was the best dancer I ever saw, too. Perhaps, my lady, you will dance with me later?''

Elizabeth modestly glanced down at her stomach. ''I shall be as clumsy as an ox.''

''Oh, I do not believe that,'' Montross interjected.

The earl gave him a sour look, obviously not pleased with his interruption. As Montross flushed, Raymond gave Elizabeth a small smile of approval.

''I do not believe that, either,'' the earl said to Elizabeth, ''and if your health permits, I would be most pleased if you would join me in a round dance.''

''I would be delighted, my lord,'' Elizabeth said. She looked at Raymond. ''My husband can play for us.''

If she had punched him in the stomach, Raymond could not have felt more winded. Play? For the earl? And dancers? ''Elizabeth,'' he growled warningly.

She came to him and took his hand, then faced the earl.

"He is too modest, my lord. He plays very well."

"So I recall," Montross muttered.

Raymond had met many men in battle. Seen the challenge in their eyes. Saw it in their stance.

This was a challenge, too. "If the earl requests it, I would be pleased to play."

Elizabeth's proud and happy smile made him glad he had agreed. "As I would be to dance. Now, come, my lord, let me show you and your wife to your quarters, so that you may refresh yourselves before the feast."

She led the couple off toward the east tower, leaving Raymond with his enemy.

Chapter Sixteen

They were not exactly alone, of course, for Cadmus sat nearby, and the earl's guard was coming into the hall, as were the servants.

"I daresay you are taken aback to see me," Montross declared.

Still challenging, and beneath the bravado, fear and uncertainty. "I knew you were rude enough that you might not answer my invitation," Raymond replied evenly.

"I was summoned by the earl."

Raymond merely raised an eyebrow at that, for that was not what Aiken's whore had said, and he would sooner believe a whore than Fane Montross.

"You may have gone too far with this marriage, Raymond. You have allied yourself to powerful men, and the earl has cause to wonder where your allegiance lies."

"The earl wonders, or you?"

"What do I care who you marry and to whom you are connected? I have allies of my own."

"You cared enough to meet her in the wood."

Montross squared his shoulders. "She told you what she thought I was after, obviously." He smiled, but it didn't extend to his eyes. "It was purely by chance—and you must think so as well, or I'm sure you would have ridden to my castle in high dudgeon and called me out."

"So that was the rest of the plan. I thought as much."

"There was no plan. You and that wife of yours—"

"You will speak of Elizabeth with respect, or you will leave, and I will tell the earl why I cast you out of my home."

Montross's gaze faltered. So, he was not sure of his footing with the earl. Otherwise, this warning would have meant nothing to him. "Your wife was mistaken," he repeated.

Raymond decided to take another tack. "I assume you have voiced your concerns about my ties by marriage to the earl."

"As I am his loyal vassal, of course I did."

"And he was so angered, he readily accepted my invitation and speaks of dancing with my wife."

"She has charmed him for the moment."

"She is very charming," Raymond agreed.

"His affability will not last."

"You still seem to find her fascinating enough to

stare at with lust in your eyes," he noted, his voice lower and more menacing.

Montross thrust out his chin. "You can't deny she is a beautiful woman."

"She is my beautiful wife."

Montross came closer, and it was clear his self-control was slipping. "A wife you don't deserve, as you didn't deserve my sister."

"You speak the truth. I didn't deserve her. I deserved better, but I didn't know what better was until Elizabeth."

Montross's eyes widened. "God's wounds," he whispered. "You love her."

His heartbeat quickening as the old fear of vulnerability came over him, Raymond said nothing.

He should have said nothing before, shown nothing, been a cipher to his enemy.

"You took my sister from me and then you killed her," Montross cried. "You don't deserve love or happiness. By God, you sicken me. You and that bitch both!"

Raymond took a step closer. "Leave Donhallow."

"I will not—not until I speak to the earl again and warn him that he is in a viper's nest here."

Raymond's anger surged, but he fought to control it. "Tell me, does the earl know that you are hiring mercenaries?"

"I am allowed to hire soldiers."

"So am I, if I feel in need of them," Raymond

replied. "But not the kind of brigands you are employing."

"The earl will understand that I need protection."

"From me, or from him?"

Montross's face flushed. "Oh, is that how this will play out? You will tell him not to trust me, when you are the traitorous one? We shall see who he believes!"

"Yes, we will."

Montross glared at him a long moment. "No, I will not stay," he snarled at last. "I won't stay here to watch you bill and coo like lovebirds, you disgusting murderer. As for the earl—"

He fell silent, perhaps realizing that he dare not disparage his overlord, no matter how upset he was.

Instead, he whirled around and marched toward the door. Every eye in the hall followed him, then the people turned their regard to Raymond, who made no sign of the unrest within.

He did not regret the confrontation. It was time Montross understood that Raymond knew about the mercenaries and so would be prepared.

Nevertheless, he was worried, too. If Montross thought he had lost the earl's favor—the one thing that had kept him in check all these years—there was no telling what the man might do.

Sitting in bed, glad to have her feet up and yawning with fatigue, Elizabeth waited for her husband to join her. He was still below, talking with the earl.

The sudden departure of Montross had caused many a raised eyebrow and whispered speculation. Elizabeth herself didn't know the exact reason why Montross had gone, but she assumed it must have been another eruption of their old enmity.

The earl had not asked any questions, suggesting to her that he likely thought the same—or thought it best to save his questions until he could be alone with Raymond.

She, too, had questions for her husband. He had not been at all surprised to see Montross ride in beside the earl. She was not surprised that Montross had come, but she was shocked to see him in the earl's cortege, which bespoke an intimacy she didn't like.

She suspected someone had forewarned Raymond, and beneath her curiosity, she was hurt. She had dared to believe that her beloved husband had come to trust her, as well as care for her. Yet if he trusted her, why would he keep secrets from her, and what else had he not told her?

At last she heard his familiar footfalls, and Cadmus panting. Deep in thought, he entered the bedchamber, while Cadmus took his place outside the door.

"Raymond?"

He started. "You are not asleep?"

"No."

"You should be," he said, coming to the bed and sitting on it. He studied her. "You look tired."

"I am tired, but I couldn't sleep until I spoke with you."

He rose and began to disrobe.

"I have to speak with you."

"About Montross," he agreed as he pulled off his tunic.

"Yes, about him. You weren't surprised to see him arrive with the earl."

He didn't answer right away. Instead, he continued to undress, sitting on the bed and pulling off a boot.

"Raymond?"

"I knew he had gone to meet the earl in London, and that he would probably journey here with him."

Elizabeth shifted toward him. "Why didn't you tell me?"

"I didn't want to alarm you," he replied without looking at her as he drew off the other boot, "especially since you are with child."

"Do you think I am so easily frightened?"

He straightened. "I saw no need to worry you over something that might not happen."

"You worry a great deal over my safety in childbirth, and there may very well be no need for that."

"This is different."

"No, it isn't, and for a man so concerned about my health, I am surprised it did not occur to you that a shock like that could send me into labor."

He twisted toward her, and on his face was an

expression of such horror, she instantly hastened to reassure her. "It didn't."

He shifted so that he faced her and gently cupped her chin in his hand. "I should have thought of that."

She took hold of his hand and regarded him steadily. "I was more hurt to think you would not tell me something so important."

"Truly, I didn't want to upset you."

"But it must have worried you, knowing that Montross was with the earl and likely spreading malicious lies. I am your wife, Raymond, and I want to share your worries. You don't have to bear them by yourself any more."

"It is a habit hard to break."

"It is not a habit," she replied. She lifted his hand and pressed a kiss upon his palm. "It is fear."

He pulled his hand away.

"An understandable fear. You trusted Allicia, and she betrayed you. I had hoped that you had come to trust me and to believe I would never betray you. Was I wrong to have that hope?"

"I do trust you."

Such simple words, and yet she thrilled to hear them, especially accompanied as they were by the look in his eyes which told her he meant what he said.

"If you are not too tired to come with me, I shall prove it."

"Where?"

"It is a secret."

"Is it far?"

"No."

"Then I am not too tired."

He rose and helped her to her feet, then went to the chest, pulling out their cloaks. Silently, she took hers and wrapped it about her, as did he.

"What will we say to the sentries?" she asked as he took one of the candles from beside the bed.

"We are not going outside," he replied, taking her hand. He broke his grasp to open the door.

Cadmus lumbered to his feet, looking at his master expectantly. "Stay, Cadmus," Raymond quietly ordered.

"He looks disappointed," Elizabeth noted as the dog settled despondently on his haunches.

"Shhh," Raymond cautioned as he started down toward the hall.

When they were halfway there, he stopped and scanned the wall. She had no idea what he was doing, until he pointed to a small nick in one of the stones at waist height. "Remember that mark," he whispered. Then he pushed on the stone, and it, as well as the three beside it and those reaching to the floor, swung open.

"It's a door," Elizabeth gasped as a cold draft of air hit her. She peered inside and saw a very narrow set of steps leading downward into total darkness. The rough walls glistened wetly in the feeble light of the single candle.

"A secret passage. Where does it lead?"

"It runs along the outer wall down to the moat, then under it. It opens in the wood on the other side."

"So far!"

"The door in the wood is concealed by a holly thicket."

She straightened. "It is amazing."

"It is for escape. My father showed it to me shortly before he died. I have never told anyone, not even Allicia."

Elizabeth's heart swelled with joy and gratitude. What more proof of his trust could she desire? For she realized that, although he did not say it, a man could enter Donhallow by this route, too. Or a troop of men, and take it from within. "Are you certain Allicia didn't know about this? A lover could sneak inside this way."

"I did think of that, and as soon as I could go out alone, I checked the other door. It didn't look as if it had been opened."

"Oh."

"But that does not mean I am absolutely sure it was not."

She nodded. "I will keep this secret, Raymond."

"I know," he said. He reached into the opening and pulled on the door, removing his hand quickly as it swung shut with a dull thud. He ran his gaze over her. "You're cold."

"Yes, I am," she admitted, wrapping her arms about herself.

"Let us go back to bed."

She took his hand and together they returned. When they were underneath the warm coverings, he rolled on his side and looked at her, his gaze intense. "I am going to tell you something, Elizabeth, that I have never told another soul. About Allicia and her brother."

Elizabeth's brow furrowed with puzzlement.

"They were always close—too close. I should have paid more heed to that, and other things, before we married."

"What are you implying, Raymond?"

"What you think," he answered softly. "There were hints, signs, warnings that their relationship was an unnatural one, but I was blind—willfully so, I think. I thought I loved Allicia, and wanted to believe her perfect."

"Until the day she tried to kill you."

"Yes. We were hunting that day, Fane and Allicia and I, with a troop of my men. They shared a secret joke, one of many, and I was annoyed at being ignored. When we returned home, I said something about them being more like lovers than siblings. It was half in jest, but I have wondered since if a part of me did not want to find out the truth."

Sighing, Raymond rolled back and looked at the ceiling. "Perhaps I wanted her to deny it. But she didn't. She didn't say a word. That night, she tried to kill me. I believe she was afraid I was going to tell people, perhaps even demand an annulment.''

"She would do murder to cover up her sin? She would have been accused and tried.''

"She might have preferred risking that, or assuming such risk as it was. Her brother would have stood by her had she claimed self-defense. I do not doubt that whatever story she told would have softened the hearts of any man who heard her, too,'' he said bitterly. "As you have seen, I have a temper. She would have used that in her defense.''

Despite the warmth of the covers and Raymond's body, Elizabeth shivered. "It sounds so...so disgusting.''

"Yet it is the only explanation I have for what Allicia did.''

"Why have you never accused Montross?''

"No proof. It would be my word against his, and until I married you, he had more influence than I.''

"You could tell the earl now.''

He shifted and looked at her sorrowfully. "Although I never loved Allicia as I do you, Elizabeth, I did care for her. Montross is ruining his own life, for he is fast losing the earl's support, and when that happens, he will lose all. I don't want to drag Allicia's memory through the mud if there is no need.''

Elizabeth caressed his rough cheek. "You are a chivalrous man, Raymond—another reason I love you.''

He turned his head and kissed her palm, causing another kind of shiver to run through her body.

But she had more questions yet, she reminded herself. "Why did Montross leave so suddenly?"

"We quarreled."

"What about?"

His gaze searched her face. "Are you certain you wish to know all?"

"Yes, Raymond, I am."

"He is hiring mercenaries, battle-hardened, Aiken tells me, and more like brigands."

"You told the earl?"

"Yes."

"What did he say to that?"

"That Montross is within his rights."

"What reason does Montross have to hire such men?"

"To protect himself from me, apparently."

Elizabeth sat up so abruptly, the baby kicked in protest. She winced.

Raymond sat up, too. "What is it?"

"The babe kicked, that's all," she explained before going on to the important thing. "Protection from you? You are not threatening him!"

"So I told the earl. And the earl is not a fool, Elizabeth. Indeed, I don't think he trusts any of his vassals completely—which is wise, really. He will keep close watch on Montross, and me, too, in all likelihood."

"*You?*"

"Yes," Raymond whispered as a smile grew on his face and he drew her back down to nestle beside him. "I have made excellent alliances with my clever marriage, you see, and he might wonder about my loyalty."

"But you are loyal and—"

"Yes, my love, and so he shall discover as time goes on. However," he murmured as he traced her lips with his fingertip, "I am weary of talking about the earl and Montross."

"As you wish, Raymond," she agreed, toying with a lock of his hair. "It has been a long day, so no doubt you wish to sleep."

"Yes, I do." His eyes gleamed with seductive mischief. "But not right away."

Chapter Seventeen

Four months later, on a cool October day, Rual glanced at the purse full of coins in Fane Montross's hand. "The babe will come within the fortnight, the village midwife says."

Fane had come alone to meet his spy, as he always did. It was easy enough for one lone man who knew it well to venture onto Raymond's land. "You are certain?"

"I was there," Rual assured him. "I heard her with my own ears. Kirkheathe has sent for a midwife from Chesney to tend to her."

"Good."

"I don't understand you," Rual muttered as she put out her hand for the payment. "Why wait till now to have your vengeance?"

"Perhaps for the same reason you are still here."

"You expect to be paid?" Rual scoffed.

Fane Montross's smile was as cold as the wind that blew down from the north. "Because I want him to suffer. I could wait until his brat is about to be born, to let him love his bride even better than he did my sister. Then, when he has lost his beloved wife, he will understand something of the anguish I felt when he murdered Allicia.''

Rual shifted uncomfortably, as if his plan seemed more cold-blooded than she had expected, or as if she was having second thoughts. ''What are you going to do?''

''Nothing that you need trouble yourself with,'' he said with another smile.

''If you're planning to attack Donhallow, I want to be well away before you do.''

''I understand, and I will ensure that you are.''

''Good. Now give me my money. I may be missed if I'm not back soon.'' She took a step toward him. He backed away and put the purse behind his back.

''What excuse did you give for coming into the woods today?''

She pointed at the basket on the ground nearby. ''I've been gathering roots to make a poultice for my lady's aching back.''

''Excellent. You always struck me as a clever woman, Rual.''

''Clever enough to know when to keep my mouth shut,'' she said, obviously intending to reassure him as to her ability to keep silent about their conspiracy.

''Tell me, does Lady Kirkheathe ever speak of me?''

"No."

"Not even a mention of my name?"

"Never to me."

"I see."

"I don't, and I don't want to. All I want is my money."

He held out the purse. "Far be it from me to keep a woman waiting," he said with a smile.

Rual cautiously reached out to take it. Before she could, Fane grabbed her wrist with his other hand and let the purse drop as he drew his dagger.

Wild-eyed and panting frantically, Rual struggled to escape his grip.

His jaw clenched, Fane pulled her inexorably closer. "You see, Rual, you don't have to worry about anything any more."

Then, his teeth bared like a rat, he thrust the dagger into her side.

Staring with disbelief, her eyes already going glassy, Rual's breath left her body in a long gasp and she began to slip slowly down to the ground, her body's weight tugging on his hand.

"I must draw him out at last, you see," he explained as she lay dying. "When he rides out to attack me, that is when I shall strike."

He let go of her hand and she fell the rest of the way with a thud. Dead or dying, he didn't care.

First he retrieved his purse. Then, as he had planned, he did what was necessary to make it look as if she had been beaten, raped and murdered.

* * *

"Are you alone, my lord?"

At the sound of his wife's voice, Raymond smiled and raised his eyes from the supply lists he was studying. The harvest had been an excellent one, and they should easily have enough food and money to get them through the winter.

Indeed, it had been one of the best summers of his life, if not the best of all. There had been no more word of additional mercenaries arriving at Montross's castle, so Raymond had cause to hope he had realized the error of his ways—and that he would do well to leave Raymond alone.

Best of all, though, was the presence of Elizabeth in his life. It was as if she had brought sunshine and music, joy and ease, and released him from the dungeon in which he had imprisoned himself.

She opened the door farther and walked into the room, swaying with the weight and bulk of her unborn child as if she were on the rocking deck of a ship.

As he studied her pale face, his eyes narrowed. "What is it?" he demanded, rising quickly. "Are you ill? Or is it time?"

"Neither," she replied, easing herself into a chair. "I am worried."

"About the baby?"

She shook her head. "No, you worry about that enough for both of us," she said with a wry smile that quickly gave way to her former seriousness. "It is Rual. She hasn't come back yet, and the sun is setting.''

Raymond glanced out the window and realized she was right. "Where did she go?"

"To the woods. As you know, my back has been a little sore, and she said she could make a salve to ease it. She wanted to go to the wood to find some roots. The day was fine, and I had no need of her, so I said she could go."

"By herself?"

"I suggested she take a guard with her, but she was most indignant. She said she would not go far, and that she knows these woods better than anyone, so she would be perfectly safe." Her brows knit with dread. "She went just after the noon. I thought she would be back long ago. Then I told myself she must have met a friend in the village and fell to talking. Then several friends.

"But now, with the sun going down, I fear she has come to some harm. I should have insisted she take a soldier, or at least one of the other servants."

Raymond came around the table and knelt before her, looking lovingly into her eyes. "She may have lost track of time in the village, or it could be that she's had a fall or some such thing in the wood. I'll send some men out searching for her. Do you know which way she went?"

Elizabeth shook her head. "No. I didn't even ask."

"Don't upset yourself," he cautioned. "We'll find her."

"I hope so!"

"As she said, she has gone into the woods often before," he reminded Elizabeth gently.

"She's never been late before. It will soon be time for the evening meal. I should have told you before now."

"She is a grown woman, not a child," he replied. "I will send out some men now. I'm sure she'll either return on her own, or they'll find her before dark."

Elizabeth put both hands on the arm of the chair and heaved herself to her feet. "I hope you're right, my love."

He put his hands lightly upon her shoulders and gazed intently into her eyes. "Rest, or you will make yourself ill with worry."

"I'll try, my love, I'll try."

"I'll take you to our room."

"I can manage that," she said with a hint of her usual fire. "You find Rual."

They did not find Rual before the sun set. Elizabeth spent a nearly sleepless night worrying about her, while Raymond didn't sleep at all, as concerned about his fretting wife as he was about the missing maidservant.

Lying on the bed nestled in his arms, Elizabeth

finally nodded off near dawn. When he was sure she was asleep, Raymond rose to lead the search anew.

Cadmus nudged the dead woman's body with his nose. He had led them to this spot, and to this terrible discovery.

Seated upon his horse near the ruined hut, Raymond cursed softly, then called his dog to him.

This was not what he wanted to find. He wanted to discover Rual at a friend's house in the village or at worst, with a broken leg or some other injury that had prevented her from returning to the castle, forcing her to spend the night in the woods. To be sure, that would have been bad enough, given the autumn chill, but this was much, much worse.

He cursed silently. He had truly let down his guard, grown slack in his duty and in the patrols of his land. It was no wonder they had been caught unawares.

That Rual, or any woman, should have to pay the price for his negligence...

"Stay, Cadmus," he ordered quietly as he dismounted and joined the group of soldiers who broke ranks and gathered round Rual.

She lay on her back, her face battered, her clothing torn so her bare breasts were exposed, her legs splayed apart. Telltale signs of a man's presence were smeared on her legs. A covered basket lay on its side nearby.

It was a horrible way for a woman to die, cruel and barbarous, robbing her of dignity as well as life.

He didn't want to have to tell Elizabeth about this.

Raymond removed his cloak and covered the body, then his gaze swept over the men. "There is no need to speak of rape when we return," he said. "Let Rual have some dignity in death, at least for now."

His men glanced at one another uncertainly.

"The whole truth must be known when we catch the lout who did this and he is tried for it, but I would spare my wife for a little while."

He walked around the body, then knelt in the mud on Rual's left side and examined her bloody bodice. In a moment, he found a rip in the cloth.

She had been stabbed, a mortal wound beneath her ribs struck by a right-handed man, likely when he was finished with her, leaving no witness to speak against him.

He sighed heavily. "Put the body on my horse."

A subdued Hale quietly detailed some men to do that necessary task. They picked up the corpse and carried it to Castor.

Castor shivered and his nostrils flared with the scent of death, yet he allowed the men to lay Rual's body across the saddle.

Meanwhile, Raymond began to examine the ground where her body had been. It had rained yesterday morning, and it looked as if the mud had been too churned up by hooves to say how many horses had been there, or how many men. Perhaps it was more than one. A roving band of brigands.

Or battle-hardened mercenaries trespassing on his land.

"Hale!"

"My lord?"

"Your best hunter."

"Derrick!" the serjeant barked, and a young man hurried toward them.

"How many men?"

Derrick regarded the ground intently, then shrugged. "Hard to say."

"Go farther afield and when you have a number, tell me."

The man bowed his head. "Aye, my lord."

"Don't go alone."

"Here, you, Martin and Rob," Hale called out to two soldiers, "go with Derrick and keep your eyes open."

The two men joined Derrick, who studied the ground a moment, then led them away along the path.

"A bad business this, my lord," Hale noted in a whisper. "Ain't had nothing like this in years."

"No, thank God," Raymond muttered.

Then he spotted something shining in the mud. He leaned over and picked up a silver coin.

It couldn't be Rual's. Even if she had silver, she would hardly carry it into the woods with her.

Maybe in her struggle, Rual had torn off her attacker's purse and spilled the contents. Gathering them up, one might have been missed.

In her struggle.

That was what seemed odd.

He looked at the ground again, particularly the indentation where her body had lain. The ground around it bore many footprints.

None of them were smeared as if she had twisted and fought.

There were no deep ruts from her kicking ankles.

He could remember no bruises on her arms where she would have been held.

Had she been stabbed first? If so, why beat her head so badly? That wound in her side would have nearly killed her at once, and certainly left her without the strength to defend herself.

If she was not fighting, would she have torn off a purse?

Or was this something else entirely?

Perhaps she had come here to meet someone. A lover? He had never noticed Rual paying special attention to any man, or a man to her, which did not mean that she was celibate. Maybe this was yet another sign of his lack of supervision of his people.

Or did the coin indicate something else? Maybe she had been selling something she had carried there in the basket. It could be she had stolen something from the hall to sell.

He strode to the basket, picked it up and pulled away the cover. Inside were some dirt-covered roots.

These must be the roots she needed to make the salve for Elizabeth. Perhaps he was wrong to be so suspicious.

Or it could be that looking for roots had been an excuse to come here.

God's wounds, a woman had betrayed him once...

He stood absolutely still and recalled all he could of Rual.

What did he know of her? Almost nothing, save that she had been in Donhallow ten years and rarely smiled. She had always kept her distance with him, but so had everyone, except Elizabeth. He could hardly consider that unusual.

No, there was nothing he could say against Rual, except that she had unwisely come into the woods alone and somehow, a silver coin had been near her body.

Derrick and the other soldiers appeared, trotting down the road. Derrick reached Raymond first. Panting, he bent over, his hands on his knees.

"Only one, my lord," he gasped, looking up at Raymond. "One horse."

"One?" Raymond repeated.

"Aye, my lord. Sure as I live, just one. Lots of marks, but all from the same horse."

"Where was he from?"

"My lord?"

"From what direction?" Raymond growled impatiently.

"Sir Fane Montross's estate."

So, the varlet came from Montross's land. Raymond was not surprised.

Who on Montross's land would have silver coins? The answer came to him instantly. Montross.

He had often heard Fane say that one death could accomplish more than an armed attack. How better to terrify the people of Donhallow without risking the earl's wrath or his own men?

Maybe this was intended to be a warning, or a sign of more terror to come.

But there was no proof, beyond his own belief that Montross was capable of such villainy. This would not be nearly enough to satisfy a justice of the king's court, or the earl.

Nevertheless, Raymond silently vowed, whoever had done this, for whatever reason, he would be found.

And he would pay.

Chapter Eighteen

Elizabeth awoke and found herself alone.

Judging by the light shining in through the narrow window, Raymond must have already gone to continue the search.

She should never have allowed Rual to go alone. She should have insisted she take a guard.

Surely there was no great danger, Elizabeth thought, trying to reassure herself. Likely it would be as Raymond had said: Rual had fallen and injured herself so that she could not get back. The night had not been so terribly cold.

She heard the castle gates swing open and quickly slipped her soft shoes over her bare feet. Easing herself up, she put her feet on the floor, then padded toward the window as quickly as she could. She had to lean forward much farther now to see below into the courtyard.

A body lay over Raymond's horse. He and his equally grim men stood nearby.

"Dear God!" she gasped as she clutched the sill. "Rual." She sank to her knees and covered her face with her hands.

This should not have happened. Even alone, Rual should have been safe on their land.

Elizabeth wept quietly, until she heard the door open and Raymond's footsteps hurriedly cross the room. He put his arm about her.

"Elizabeth," he crooned huskily as he helped her stand, "it cannot be good for you to kneel on this cold stone floor."

"That is Rual on your horse, isn't it?" she asked through her tears, her anxious gaze searching his face for confirmation as he led her to the bed. She sat heavily.

Nodding, he just as anxiously studied her as he sat beside her.

"How did it happen?"

"She was attacked."

"Attacked?" Elizabeth murmured incredulously. She regarded Raymond with grim certainty. "She was raped, too, wasn't she?"

"I wasn't going to tell you about that until I had to," he confessed.

"Raymond, I was in a convent, not heaven. Some of the girls were sent there because they had been raped, and though they had not been at fault, they were exiled there to prevent a scandal. So I know very well such things happen. How far from the castle was she?"

"At the ruined hut near the river."

"But that is not far," Elizabeth protested as if that somehow made Rual's death impossible—as she wished it did.

"Yes."

"Who would do such a thing?"

"Montross."

She stared at him in horrified wonder. "Montross! But he is a knight."

"A dishonorable one."

Raymond reached into his belt and pulled out the silver coin. "I found this and that is one reason I suspect Montross."

"A coin?"

"A silver coin."

"Many men carry silver coins, even outlaws."

He nodded in acknowledgment and continued. "There were the hoof prints of only one horse coming to and from Montross's land."

"But it could have been one of his tenants or soldiers, or one of those mercenaries he hired. Surely one of them would be much more likely to be a murderer."

"I know, but I also know Montross. He could do something like this, if he thought it necessary."

"Necessary? Why would raping and killing one of our servants be necessary?"

"Did you trust Rual?"

She frowned. "Why, yes, I saw no reason not to."

He looked at the coin he twisted in his hand. "Perhaps that was a mistake."

"You think she was in league with Montross?" Elizabeth demanded as the possible significance of the coin hit her like a blast of hot air from an oven. "You think that coin was part of a payment? What could she possibly have told him?"

Raymond rubbed his weary eyes and began to count the items on his fingers. "The number of weapons we have. When and where my men will be. The contents of our storerooms. How many bowmen I have, or horses or foot soldiers." He stopped and regarded her with grim intensity. "A hundred things an enemy would find useful."

The baby within Elizabeth shifted and she placed her hand on her rounded stomach. "I still find it difficult to believe."

"I do not, perhaps because I have more experience with dishonor."

Her heart ached to hear him refer to his past. "Women's especially," she agreed. "Raymond, while you have good reason to think as you do, could it not have been an outlaw?"

"Of course, or one of Montross's men who saw an opportunity and took it."

"Would that not be a more likely explanation, considering that poor Rual was raped?"

"Yes, or else that was intended to deflect suspicion from Montross."

"But if she was his spy, why would he kill her, and why now?"

"Perhaps she was demanding too much money for her information, and he thought he had paid her enough."

"We shall look in her quarters and see if we find evidence of other payments," Elizabeth said. She watched him as he studied the coin in his hand. "You can think of another reason, can't you?"

He raised his solemn eyes to look at her, and new fear threaded down her back. "Perhaps she had outlived her usefulness to him. It could be that he believes he knows all he needs to know to move against us.

"God save us, Elizabeth," he muttered, raking his hand through his hair, "I have been too complacent. I should have known better than to think that realizing the earl was aware of his activity would stop Montross."

"Raymond," she said, taking his hand in hers, "Montross couldn't simply attack us without just cause, or the earl and even the king himself would call that treason. Even if a servant rebels against his master, it is called treason."

Raymond sighed heavily. "I am quite sure Montross will have a good explanation at the ready. Likely he will accuse me of plotting against the earl, or the king."

"Which is utterly ridiculous!"

Her husband's lips twisted into a sardonic smile.

"If Montross does plan to attack, we can be sure he has some kind of evidence at hand, or else he will find another way to deflect any serious consequence. Or it may be enough for him that I will be dead."

"Don't say such things!" Elizabeth cried, horrified by that thought. "If he attacks us, he will be the one suffering consequences, provided he even survives," she finished staunchly.

Raymond smiled and cupped her chin in his powerful fingers. "Ah, my love, I only wish it could be so simple as combat between him and me. Sadly, I fear it will not be."

As he kissed her gently, Elizabeth felt a small ache and put her hand on her side.

"What is it? Is it the baby?"

"A little pain, nothing serious."

"Are you certain?"

"As certain as you are about Montross. What are we going to do? We must do *something*, Raymond."

"Yes. We must bury Rual."

Elizabeth leaned heavily on Raymond's arm while Father Daniel said the words over Rual's grave in the village graveyard after the noon meal. It was a simple ceremony, with a few heartfelt words of blessing to lay her to rest.

Gathered around were other servants from Donhallow, and the sound of sniffing and soft weeping filled the air. Elizabeth was surprised to see such grief, for she had never thought the quiet, aloof Rual particularly well-liked. Yet was there any woman who could not find it in her heart to weep with sympathy at such an end?

Even though Elizabeth had found a purse full of more silver coins in a secret compartment of Rual's chest that was strong evidence of betrayal, she could still mourn for the way she went to God. She also thanked God that Genevieve had possessed a similar chest, with a similar compartment; otherwise, Elizabeth might never have found the purse.

The sound of horses' hooves and jingling harness interrupted the priest's quiet blessing, drawing the attention of all gathered there.

Elizabeth held even tighter to Raymond's arm as Fane Montross, accompanied by a guard of twenty rough-looking, well-armed men, rode toward the graveyard.

"My lord, my lady," he said, bowing from the back of his horse, "I hear you have had some trouble on your land."

Raymond didn't answer at once. Instead he escorted Elizabeth to the priest. "Stay with him," he commanded.

He was again as he had been that first day—just as cold, just as distant. "Raymond—"

"Do as I say," he commanded before he turned to face Montross.

She didn't want to remain with Father Daniel, yet she was heavily pregnant. What could she do but watch her husband walk toward Montross and his men?

"I heard about your maidservant," Montross said. "A terrible business. Since we are neighbors, I have come to offer my help."

"More gossip flying on the wind?" Raymond inquired.

"Is it not true?"

Raymond didn't answer.

"So it is, and I have come here to offer any assistance I can render."

"We don't want anything from you."

"No? You already know who did it?" he inquired. "You have them in custody?"

Raymond crossed his arms.

"God's wounds, Raymond, there could be a marauding band of brigands hereabouts. If you do not have them in custody, where are they?"

Again her husband said nothing.

"Or do you intend to allow them to continue murdering people? Hardly the actions of a responsible overlord. The earl will not be impressed."

In the face of Montross's mocking words and her husband's lack of response, Elizabeth could no longer remain silent. She pushed herself away from the priest and went toward them as fast as she could. "We have an excellent idea who did this."

"Elizabeth," Raymond warned in a low growl.

"My lady, how delightful to speak with you again." Montross's gaze raked her swollen body. "I can see why your husband does not care to leave your side. I must agree with the earl that being with child makes a woman even more beautiful. It is no wonder your husband is neglecting his duty to his tenants and the earl to linger in his castle with you.''

''My husband knows his duties well enough, just as he knows who killed Rual.''

''Really? If he is so certain, why does he not have him in the dungeon of Donhallow? Has the clever fellow escaped? Or could it be that you don't have enough evidence to take him into custody? Oh, what a pity if that is the case.''

''We will,'' she declared.

''Your husband doesn't seem to think so.''

Elizabeth glanced at her grave and silent husband, but she could not read the expression in his eyes any more than she could read his mind. ''We will. Soon,'' she vowed.

''Poor Raymond is struck dumb,'' Montross remarked. ''Tell me, my old friend, is there another reason you do not speak? A fear of what I might do in retaliation if you make serious and unprovable accusations, perhaps? Concern for your pretty pregnant wife who you hold so very, very dear—more dear than my poor, beautiful sister, eh?''

Elizabeth glanced sharply at Raymond. Was that so? Is that why he stood so still and silent—fear for her safety?

Two strong emotions vied within her at that moment: pride that he cared so much for her, and horror that his affection weakened him in this man's eyes.

"Please, Raymond, take me inside, away from this person. I have no more desire to be in his company."

"Yes, Raymond," Montross mocked. "Take her away, and yourself, too."

"Until another time, Montross," Raymond replied, his voice as hard and cold as iron in winter. "And get off my land."

Montross's triumphant, taunting laughter followed them as they proceeded to the castle, followed by the priest and those who had been at the burial.

"We must speak of this, my lord," Elizabeth said as they passed through the gate.

Raymond stared straight ahead. "No."

"I'm sorry if I disobeyed you, but I could not bear to hear him say those things without being called to account."

"It was not your place to do so. I told you, we need evidence before we can accuse him."

"But to let him think he is getting away with a terrible crime—!"

"To let him ramble on as he will without replying so that he knows we cannot be goaded into hasty action."

Elizabeth halted. "Oh, dear God in heaven, I never thought of that."

"I thought not." He looked at her, and she saw the concern in his eyes. "I should not walk so fast."

"It doesn't matter. Raymond, I'm sorry!"

He took her arm and steered her toward the stables. "I have a hearty dislike of discussing such matters in the courtyard," he reminded her.

As they went inside the stables, one look from her husband sent the grooms and stable boys scurrying out.

"I must know, is it as he says, Raymond? Are you loath to upbraid him for fear of what he will do?"

Raymond's brow furrowed. "I am not a coward, Elizabeth." He put his hands gently on Elizabeth's slim shoulders and regarded her steadily. And then he smiled. "Fane Montross has never been able to abide silence. I knew it would annoy him."

Her eyes widened, while he grew serious. "Elizabeth, that fool came here today to taunt me into action by threatening you, believing that my love for you and our child has made me weak. At one time, when I was just beginning to realize how much I cared for you, I feared that it would, too. Yet when he came here today and made his threats, I realized how wrong I was to think that, and so is he. My love for you does not make me weak. It makes me strong—and more determined than ever to protect those I love. Fane Montross has made a very grave error by threatening you, Elizabeth. There is nothing worse that he could have done, for I will fight for you and our child to my last breath."

"Oh, Raymond," she said, a quaver in her voice

as she looked into his eyes, "I don't want you to die for me."

"I promise you, my love," he said, caressing her cheek, "that I shall do my best to avoid it." He smiled tenderly. "Now I am going to address my men. It is time those who may have to fight with me knew all. Will you come with me, or would you rather rest?"

"I would like to go with you."

He smiled at her, pride and love shining in his dark eyes. "Come then, my lady, who once falsely assured me she could keep quiet."

When they reached the hall, they saw that many of the soldiers were there, talking nervously, along with the servants.

They all fell silent when they realized their lord and his lady had arrived, and a few began to head for the doors, either to the courtyard or the kitchen.

"Stay," Raymond commanded. The people exchanged wary glances, but did as they were told.

He led Elizabeth to a chair, where she gratefully sat, then faced the people. He took a deep breath, and spoke, the words strong, if hoarse. "You have heard what happened to Rual. Unfortunately, I have reason to suspect that Rual was not in the woods for the reason she gave to my wife, or rather, for that and something else besides. It is my belief, bolstered by what Lady Kirkheathe discovered among Rual's possessions, that she has been a spy among us."

A gasp went through the crowd, followed by mutters of disbelief and dismay.

They fell silent when Raymond raised his hand. "I also think I know who is behind it—Montross. If he did not do the actual deed, I believe he is nevertheless responsible for her death.

"But I have no proof. Until I do, I cannot bring a charge against him, and we are all in danger. I believe this man will stop at nothing to have his revenge on me for killing his sister, and for that I ask your forgiveness."

The people's eyes widened in stunned disbelief.

"Allicia's death was an accident. She attacked me and when I threw her from me, she struck her head and died.

"Even though I acted with provocation against one person trying to kill me, I have put you and all my people at risk because Montross will have his revenge." He raised his hand to his throat. "Whatever provocation Montross feels, he has no justification for murder in return.

"Yet *I must have proof,*" Raymond continued, his voice stronger. "There will be more patrols, and when you men return, tell me of anything suspicious, no matter how insignificant it might seem. If you find any stranger on the land, or one of Montross's men, you will capture them and bring them back here *unharmed* to be questioned. There must be no questionable confessions elicited by torture.

"Likewise, you will not go onto Montross's land,

not even in chase. We must be faultless, or God only knows what Montross will say.

"Sadly, I fear there may be more trouble ahead, so warn your families. They should be prepared to seek sanctuary in the castle at short notice."

"Just as long as that rat gets his just deserts!" someone called out.

"Down with Montross!" shouted another.

"Up with Kirkheathe!"

"God bless the Lady Elizabeth!" one of the soldiers cried, and the others took up the cry.

"Yes," Raymond said as he turned to her. "God bless my Lady Elizabeth."

She smiled as he came toward her. "I believe I know why you were so quiet when I first met you," she said softly, her words not carrying far in the din. "You were saving your voice for all you had to say today."

He gently tugged her to her feet, then took her in his arms for a passionate kiss, which made the people cheer even more.

"Raymond," she panted when he stopped. "In front of all these people! Indeed, my lord, I don't know what's come over you."

"It's love, Elizabeth. Love has come over me. My love for you has freed me and yes, loosened my tongue." He gave her a small, mischievous smile. "Or perhaps I only wanted them to know how pleased I am with my wife."

She returned his smile, which would be the last they would share for a long time.

Chapter Nineteen

Four days later, Elizabeth glanced uneasily at Raymond as they ate the noon meal in the crowded hall. He looked exhausted, and she was reminded that he was not a young man. He was a seasoned warrior, and one with gray hair on his head and in the stubble on his cheeks.

Cadmus lay beside him, seemingly too tired even to beg for food. Several villagers and tenants had already sought sanctuary, and they sat among weary soldiers recently back from patrolling with Raymond.

Strangers had been seen in the wood near the border between Donhallow and Montross's estate. Montross's mercenaries, they appeared to be, but unfortunately none had been captured, so they had only their own opinion about who they were, as well as why they were there.

Raymond caught Elizabeth looking at him.

"You must rest," she said, lightly resting her

hand on his knee beneath the table, ''or you will fall ill.''

''I am more concerned for you,'' he replied. ''I thought the baby would be born by now.''

''They come when they come, although I will be happy when it is over. I am almost convinced that the waiting is worse than the labor could be.''

''I would feel better if the midwife from Chesney were here.''

''She will be soon. She warned you she might be delayed tending to one of the earl's relatives. If she does not arrive in time, there is always the village midwife. She expects only one more baby soon, and when that child arrives, she can come to Donhallow until my time.''

''I pray those babes arrive quickly, then.''

''I don't know what I dread more, that Montross will attack, or that he won't.''

A young soldier ran into the hall. ''My lord!'' He hurried toward them. ''Smoke, my lord. Heavy. Rising from one of the farms.''

Raymond was on his feet in an instant. So was Cadmus, quivering with excitement.

Raymond looked down at his wife. ''I believe our wait for Montross to act is over.''

Gripping the arms of her chair, Elizabeth heaved herself up. ''Take care, my lord, my love.''

''I will. Stay,'' he ordered Cadmus, then he looked at her. ''I will feel better if he is here with you, in addition to Barden and my best men. Cadmus will protect you as well as any soldier.''

She nodded, and he kissed her on her cheek before marching from the hall, followed by his men.

When he was gone, she splayed her hands on the table and let her breath out slowly as the pain passed.

By the time Raymond and his men arrived at the farm, the byre and house were ablaze. Chickens flapped around the yard in a panic. Inside the byre, an ox bellowed.

Raymond spotted the tenant's body face down in the dirt, an arrow protruding from his back. He recognized the man. His name was Dennis, and he had a wife and children.

Turning his gaze away from the terrible sight, Raymond surveyed the yard. The attackers were long gone.

''Put out the fire,'' he commanded Hale, who immediately sent his men to form a line between the well and the house.

''Get the ox,'' he ordered another soldier close to him. The man hurried to obey.

Then, covering his mouth with his hand and squinting against the smoke, Raymond ran into the dwelling.

The woman lay beside the hearth where she had fallen, an arrow through her throat. Nearby, lying with their heads upon the table as if asleep, sat two children, a boy and a girl.

Their small throats had been cut.

Raymond had seen many dead people in his years, but no sight ever sickened him as this did.

He stumbled back outside, silently vowing that he would find the men who did this and they would face justice. He would prove who was behind this. Then he would see them all executed for murder.

A mounted patrol arrived. Every man looked horrified, and new worry creased their faces.

The leader quickly dismounted. "We saw a group of mounted men riding off toward Montross's land five miles off and gave chase, my lord," he said, his eyes full of sorrow and remorse. "They made it off your land, so we turned to go back. It was then we saw the smoke. They must have done this."

"When were you last here?"

"This morning."

"You saw nothing amiss then?"

"No, my lord, but we tried to talk Dennis into going to the castle for safety, him being so close to Montross's estate. His wife was all for it, but he said he wasn't going to be chased off by that…well, he called him that sorry bugger, my lord."

"It doesn't matter what he called him, now that he is dead."

"No, my lord, I don't suppose it does," the man replied grimly.

"Then what did you do?"

"We went on our way, to the west."

"And these men, what did they look like?"

"Tough, my lord, and well-armed. Pretty clear they were up to no good. They led us a merry chase." His gaze faltered. "I know now they was leadin' us away from here. I wish we'd come upon 'em before, not after. I'm sorry, my lord."

"I am sorry, too—but it would have been better if Dennis had listened to you. He did not." He regarded the mournful soldier intently. "Would you recognize any of those men again?"

"One of 'em I would," he said firmly. "Big ugly brute with a scar."

"Good."

"My lord!" one of the soldiers cried, pointing east over the trees toward another plume of thick dark smoke rising in the sky.

"And there!" cried another, gesturing to the west.

After the instant of shock had passed, fierce and righteous anger surged through Raymond. Montross had to be behind a series of attacks and by God, he would pay!

"You, take your patrol to the west," he commanded the leader of the second group to arrive. "The rest, with me to the east."

They mounted and rode, and Raymond hoped they would not be too late to prevent more bloodshed. Please, God, he silently prayed, let me not be too late—and let Montross be there!

But Montross was not at either farm.

He was headed elsewhere.

*   *   *

Elizabeth's eyes snapped open as another pain assaulted her body. The pangs were too strong and came too regularly, albeit far apart, for her to think she was not in labor. She clenched her teeth and waited for the pain to pass.

The babe was ready to come into the world, whether it was a good time or not, but perhaps not for some hours yet.

The midwife had told her first labors usually took a long while. These days, Raymond was happiest— or at least the least troubled—when he was patrolling. Let him come home in his own time. There was no urgent need to summon him yet, surely.

There was a noise outside, like the rushing of the wind, or rain falling.

"My lady!" Greta called out as she pounded on the bedchamber door. "My lady, they've attacked the outlying farms."

Beside the bed, Cadmus got to his feet and barked.

"Attacked the farms?" Elizabeth repeated as the pain ebbed. "Quiet, Cadmus."

He stopped barking as she eased herself to her feet and made her way to the door.

Greta looked too frightened even to cry. "They've attacked at least three farms, my lady," she exclaimed. "You can see the fires." Her whole arm trembling, Greta pointed at the window.

Elizabeth slowly went to look, grabbing the sill to steady herself. Greta was right; smoke from three fires rose in the distance. And the noise she heard was the babble of panicked voices as equally frightened villagers and their livestock streamed into the courtyard.

Where was Raymond? And the patrols? Had they been attacked? Lured out of the castle and set upon by Montross and his mercenaries?

As Greta started to weep, Elizabeth made a decision. No one must know she was in labor. Not yet. Not while this was going on. She had plenty of time before the baby would come. The midwife had said so.

Elizabeth wanted to speak to Barden and do what must be done to protect Donhallow and its people; when all was as secure as possible, she would summon the midwife, who might even be here already, with the others.

Reassured by that thought, she turned toward Greta.

"When were the fires spotted?"

"A moment ago. Barden sent me here right away to tell you."

"I must speak to him."

Greta looked at Elizabeth's swollen belly, then her face. "My lady, are you sure? He can come—"

"Take me to the hall, then send for him."

Greta, calmer now, did as she was told and helped

her to the hall, one wary eye on Cadmus all the while.

Once there, Elizabeth sent a soldier to ask Barden to come to the hall.

Another pain struck her while she waited and she struggled to betray no hint of her agony. She had hidden her pain many times before in the convent; she would do so now until things were under control.

When he still did not come, she said to Greta, "Help me to the door. I will go to Barden. No doubt he is too busy to come to me."

They reached the door just as Barden dashed up the steps. The noise in the courtyard was overwhelming as frightened people milled around uncertainly. More were rushing through the gates, carrying bundles and leading animals, so that the gate was jammed.

"Are all the patrols still out?"

"Yes, my lady."

"Have you sent out any reinforcements?"

"No, my lady."

"Do so."

Barden shook his head. "I regret, my lady, that Lord Kirkheathe told me that under no circumstances was I to send out more men. We are to guard Donhallow, no matter what."

Elizabeth chewed her lip in frustration. The patrols were twenty men at most; if Montross sent a large force against them, it would not be good, even if Raymond's men joined together to fight him.

Yet Raymond had given this man a direct command that she was sure Barden would not disobey.

"How many more people are coming to the castle?"

The commander glanced back. "Too many. We cannot close the gates, my lady, and we must."

"Not yet," she said, thinking of the families desperately hurrying to get inside. "Surely the patrols can hold the attackers away from the village."

Even if they all died.

Even if Raymond died.

She mustn't think of that. Her duty now was to see to her people in their hour of need, and save as many of them as she could.

"My lady, we *must* close the gates."

"A little more time," she insisted. She sucked in her breath as another pain hit her.

"My lady, are you—?"

"I am fine. Send some of your men to hurry the people. Tell them no more animals. Oxen are too slow."

"What if they won't leave their livestock?"

The pain ebbed, replaced by a different sort of ache as she felt the full impact of what it meant to be the chatelaine of a castle at such a time. "Tell them that we must close the gates at once and the courtyard is too full as it is. If they still refuse, give them this choice: leave the animals, or stay outside to die with them.''

Awe flared in Barden's cool gray eyes. "Yes, my lady.''

"Go now, and give the orders.'' She made a small, compassionate smile. "I think most of them will decide to live.''

He turned on his heel, then glanced back. "My lord chose his wife well,'' he said.

There was a sound, a hiss of air—and then an arrow struck Barden in the chest. Greta screamed, a high-pitched screech that rent the air. Elizabeth, too shocked to make a sound, watched in horror as Barden fell to his knees, then tumbled down the steps.

The crowd in the courtyard erupted into pandemonium. People screamed, shouted, sobbed and tried to run inside whatever building was nearest. Elizabeth grabbed Greta and, despite her pain, grabbed hold of her arm to keep her from running away in panic. More men were pouring in through the gate and joining with hers in combat.

Somebody grabbed her arm, and tugged them both back into the hall.

It was Aiken, white to the lips. A group of women and children had also taken refuge there and they huddled together. Despite their silence, their pale faces and wide eyes told Elizabeth they were terrified.

She wanted to say something, to reassure them, but at that moment, another pain assailed her. She pressed her lips together and tried to stay on her feet, forcing herself to think, as duty demanded.

Greta, however, fell to her knees, sobbing.

Elizabeth ignored her and as soon as she felt able to speak, she addressed Aiken. "Who is in command now?"

"I don't know, my lady," Aiken replied, glancing down at his wife.

"Then you are."

He looked up at her swiftly. "My lady?"

"I put you in command of Donhallow until my lord returns."

The man nodded, and she was pleased to see that color returned to his cheeks. "I will do my best, my lady."

"I know it."

"No!" Greta wailed.

"I must have a good man in charge," Elizabeth said, trying to be kind, but more determined that Aiken take command of the men outside.

"After I leave," he said firmly, "close these doors and let no one in. Fetch water from the kitchen in case they try to fire the roof."

Another pain, the worst yet, struck Elizabeth and she held to the wall, panting and hoping she wouldn't swoon. She couldn't swoon.

Nor could she stay here, or people would know she was in labor. They had other things to concern them now. They had to save Donhallow, just as she had to protect her unborn child. Raymond's child.

Yet it was her duty to offer leadership to her people until Raymond returned, especially to those in the hall once Aiken was gone.

She could not do that while this agony gripped her.

"I'm leaving you now, my lady," Aiken said, "and I give you my word—my lady, what is it?"

"I have to lie down."

"Greta, help my lady."

The sobbing woman got to her feet and wiped her nose.

Elizabeth waved her off as the pain subsided. "Stay here and help the others until Aiken's orders have been carried out," she said with all the authority she could muster. The last thing she wanted now was Greta, with her terror-stricken eyes and nervous hands.

Greta mercifully obeyed.

"Come, Cadmus," Elizabeth said, putting her hand on his large head for support.

They slowly began to make their way toward her bedchamber.

She hoped her people would later understand why she seemed to be abandoning them. She had no choice.

Surely they would be safe in the hall. And the rest of the tenants and villagers, too. Montross would be a fool to kill them, or who would work the estate and pay his tithes, supposing he wrested control of it from Raymond, which he could only do by killing him—

At that thought, a cry of anguish broke from her lips. Montross *was* a fool, the kind of fool who would kill for revenge. The kind of fool who would get at a man through his wife, or his child.

She splayed her hand on the wall at the onset of a spasm and closed her eyes. Below, she could hear the movement of furniture as the women blockaded the door. There was nothing more she could do here.

"Please, God, protect us all, and let them give us time," she murmured, knowing what she had to do.

She had to protect her baby.

As the pain passed and she opened her eyes, she spotted the nick. She pushed and the little door to the passage swung open.

Dear God, how was she going to get through that?

She must, and she would.

Cadmus nuzzled her leg.

She needed time. Time to get away. Time to hide. Time to bear her child away from here.

If Montross and his men thought she was still in Donhallow…

"Cadmus, sit." The dog did as she ordered, although his whole body quivered and his bottom barely touched the ground.

"Cadmus, stay."

He started to whimper and inched forward.

"Stay!"

Holding the wall for support, she slowly knelt and

turned around so that she would be moving backward through the opening and down the slick, narrow steps. If she stood, or even tried to stand, she might slip and fall, or faint.

With one hand protecting her belly, she crawled back through the door, nearly gagging on the fetid air.

It was going to be dark, too.

There was no other way. She had to protect Raymond's baby.

Once more she looked at the anxious dog. "Stay, Cadmus," she whispered softly. "That's a good dog."

Then she pushed the door closed.

Chapter Twenty

"Run!"

The warning cry went up from the attackers as Raymond and his men rode toward the burning cottage.

Raymond could see at least five men, including one holding down a struggling young woman and another on top of her fumbling with her skirts.

One hand holding his reins, his teeth bared like a wild animal, Raymond reached for his sword and drew it in one fluid motion as he bore down upon them.

The man holding the woman let go of her and joined his comrades fleeing into the wood. The other struggled to his feet, trying to pull up his breeches at the same time.

Raymond forgot what he said about taking these men alive.

In the next moment, the would-be rapist's head

rolled away from his falling body while the terrified woman screamed.

Raymond barely took note as he urged Castor into the wood after the men. His soldiers likewise scattered in chase.

He would get them all. Kill them all.

Where were they? His shoulders heaving as he breathed in great gasps of air, he drew his horse to a halt and listened. He heard his men, their shouts and the clang of sword on sword.

His pulse still racing, he commanded himself to be calm and *think.* The brigands were not going to escape and by God, they would tell him who had ordered them here. They would incriminate Montross. These attacks were too bold and too numerous to be anything but a concerted attack by his enemy, who was probably comfortably back in his castle, ready to deny any wrongdoing. He would likely say the men acted without his leave, and then—

Raymond's heart leaped to his throat and he couldn't breathe.

For what if Montross were *not* in his castle. What if these attacks were a feint, intended to lure him out of Donhallow, so that Montross could—

Raymond opened his mouth to shout to his men to return.

He couldn't shout. He hadn't been able to yell since Allicia had ruined his voice. He couldn't call to his men to join him and get back to Donhallow.

But he could not wait.

* * *

Soon, very soon, Raymond D'Estienne was going to know what real torment was, Fane thought with a satisfied smile as he crept up the slick steps, a torch in his hand to light the way up the secret passage. Soon, very soon, he was going to know how it felt to lose someone you loved with your whole heart, as Raymond had never loved Allicia.

If he had, he wouldn't have been able to kill her.

He was so close to having his vengeance on Raymond! Indeed, after all these years, the waiting outside the village until he heard his mercenaries breach the gates of Donhallow had been nearly unbearable.

But they had, and now they were doing what they liked inside Raymond's castle.

And these were not the few mercenaries Raymond and the earl knew about. These were different men, hired and paid in secret, carefully chosen, kept far away until it was nearly time for Raymond's wife to bear his brat. He had contact with only one of the outlaws, a disgusting, violent man he had found in London long ago. This way, if they were caught looting Donhallow, only one could name Montross—one outlaw, whose word could never stand up before the courts. The louts could take whatever they wanted from Donhallow and kill anybody who tried to stop them, once they had taken the lady of Donhallow to her bedchamber and locked her in, alone.

Oh, yes, Fane thought with satisfaction even as the sweat trickled down his back, he had planned and chosen well. All Raymond would know was that *someone* had killed his wife and unborn child. Let him suspect all he wanted; without proof, there was nothing he could do, which would add to his hell on earth.

Fane's foot slipped and he put out his free hand to steady himself. The walls were as damp and slimy as the steps, and his lip curled with revulsion as he wiped his palm off on his breeches.

One night Allicia had stumbled just like this as she went up the tower steps. She had put out her hand, as he had just done, and found the opening. The next day, she had taken a candle and investigated, going the full way down to the exit in the holly bushes. She had never told Raymond of her discovery, just as he had not shared this secret with her.

That had upset her greatly, and Fane had hoped she would finally realize that Raymond did not truly love her, not as he did.

She must have known that. After all, she confided this secret to her dear brother when he came to stay the night before going on a hunt. She had wanted to see Fane without anybody else knowing, and he was to join her in the solar when all were asleep.

It would be like old times again, he had thought joyously, when they had comforted one another, often sharing the same bed when their brute of a father had been on one of his rampages. Then one night, when Fane was fourteen and Allicia twelve, their comfort had taken a different form.

No, she could never love anyone as she loved him, just as he could never love any other woman the way he loved her. He was not ashamed of that, nor had Allicia been, although they both knew they dare not disclose what had happened. People would not understand that theirs was a special love.

And then Raymond had fallen in love with her.

Fane scowled as he recalled how Allicia had altered as Raymond came between them. Even now, he wanted to growl with jealousy…but then she had missed *him* so much that she begged him to come to her.

How happy she had been to see him! She had tried not to show it. She even tried to sound cold and distant—because she was afraid. Not of him. Never of him. Of her husband, the church and what people—especially Raymond the righteous—would say, but not him.

And then she had confessed that she feared Raymond suspected the truth.

How could he, Fane had demanded, unless she told him. *He* never would.

Still she had persisted, claiming she couldn't live with the shame if he did. She was so upset, she had not even wanted him to touch her, but he had persisted. Finally she had stopped struggling and let him comfort her again. Even if she tried to deny it, that was what she really wanted, what she truly needed, to be in his arms again.

Raymond could never take her loving brother's place.

That's why she had tried to kill Raymond the next night—to get away from him, and to keep their secret. If she had succeeded, they would have been together forever.

But Raymond had killed her.

So now he would kill Raymond's wife, whom Raymond so obviously adored, and the unborn child within her.

Finally Fane reached the end of the passage. Now the hour of his triumph was at hand. Now he would make Raymond pay. Now he would know how it felt to lose the person he held most dear in all the world.

With a smile, Fane put his hand on the door and pushed it open. He pinched out the candle's flame, drew his sword and came out onto the tower stairs.

Then Fane Montross looked up and saw Raymond's huge hound staring down at him, growling, his teeth bared and his whole body tensed to spring.

Panting, the pain continuous, Elizabeth rested on her hands and knees for a moment, trying to think beyond the agony.

You have been in pain before, she told herself. You can—

A groan escaped her lips.

How much longer before the baby came? What was she going to do, out here in the wood all alone?

What if the baby wasn't turned the right way? What if she bled to death before they were found?

She had no idea how far she was from Donhallow, so she had to keep going. She had to get away from the men attacking her home.

Where was Raymond? Was he all right?

He must be. He would defeat Montross and his men and then he would find her.

He had to win. If he died, she would suffer as she had never suffered before.

He must live. He would live. He and his men would defeat the attackers, and all would be well. She would not think otherwise.

Would the pain never end?

She moaned again as another forceful contraction took her and she fell to the ground, curling up and holding her stomach as if that could somehow help. She pressed her lips together tightly so she wouldn't make any louder noise.

How long she lay thus, lost in her pain, anxious and afraid, she couldn't be sure.

It started to rain. She could feel it on her face and head.

Somewhere, somehow, she had lost her scarf.

Another brutal pain took her.

Even in her torment, she knew she couldn't stay here out in the open, sheltered only by the trees.

With a low groan, she crawled to a tree and, pressing against it, managed to get to her feet.

"Oh, dear God," she moaned, her eyes closed as she struggled for the strength to stand. "Help me."

She took a few steps, then fell to her knees, breaking the fall with her hands.

Gasping, trying to breathe, she raised her head as the rain began falling faster, the drops soaking her through.

She had to find shelter.

Again she fought to stand, yet couldn't straighten.

Her hands on her knees, she raised her eyes, and there, through the rain and the trees, she saw a farmer's cottage.

She could make that, she told herself. If she did, they would be safe. There would be help.

Elizabeth struggled onward, sometimes staggering forward, sometimes on her hands and knees, her soaked and muddy gown clinging to her body.

Occasionally she had to stop, resisting the urge to scream in agony as the pain seemed to squeeze the very breath from her.

And then, as she leaned on the post of a small fence surrounding a pigsty, her water broke, rushing down her legs in an unfamiliar torrent.

"Oh, God," she moaned as the pig squealed.

Where was the farmer and his family? Why hadn't anybody seen her and come to her aid?

The answer came to her as she looked at the cottage with shutters over its windows.

They weren't there.

They must have gone to Donhallow for safety

when they saw the smoke, guessing it meant an attack upon the estate.

At least there would be shelter here.

There had to be shelter here. She had to get inside, out of the rain.

Clenching her teeth as the pain ripped through her, she dragged herself into the yard.

As the rain began to fall, Raymond tore his way through the holly bushes.

He had to get inside Donhallow, and without his men to back him, he must take the secret way. He had no candle or torch to light his way, but that would not deter him.

There. He was at the door. Quickly he pulled down on the latch and yanked it open.

He would leave it ajar to give him a little light.

Even that disappeared all too soon and he had to feel his way upward, mindful of the slippery rock beneath his feet as his hands brushed over the slick walls.

He thought he would never get to the end, but at last, his toe struck the door at the end of the passage. He drew his sword from his scabbard. Then, with his left hand, he felt for the latch that would open the secret door.

Something blocked the way.

He shoved harder and the door opened a crack to reveal something bloody lying on the ground. A small man?

He saw a patch of familiar fur.

Cadmus. God save him, Cadmus lay across the threshold. If Cadmus was dead, what of Elizabeth?

Raymond put his shoulder to the door and with one mighty push, got it open. Below, he could hear a rhythmic thudding.

Someone was trying to break down the door of the hall with a battering ram.

Raymond ignored the noise. As long as the door held, there was nothing he could do. Instead, his gaze scanned poor Cadmus, his body cut in several places, the floor around him covered in blood. Boot prints went upward, toward the bedchamber.

Raymond stepped over Cadmus's body and dashed toward the bedchamber. The door was open.

His heart pounding, he ran into the room—to see Montross sitting on the floor by the window, leaning against the wall. His tunic was red with blood, his face gashed, his lips nearly as pale as his cheeks, his eyes closed. His chest rose and fell with his labored breathing.

Raymond felt not a particle of pity as he strode across the room, grabbed him by his tunic and hauled him to his feet. Montross's sword fell to the floor with a clang and his eyes slowly opened.

"Where is my wife?" Raymond demanded, his nose inches from his enemy's sweaty face.

"I don't know."

Raymond shook him. He was as limp as a doll.

"Liar! I left my dog to protect her and he lies dead."

Montross weakly struggled in his grasp. "And he has killed me," he whispered.

Raymond glared at him, and Montross slowly nodded his head. "I am bleeding to death."

Only then did Raymond see that Montross's arm had nearly been torn from his body, and the puddle of blood.

"He died for nothing, that dog. He attacked me, but she was already gone."

Raymond let go of him and, holding his arm, Montross slumped back against the wall.

The passage. She must have gone out by the passage.

Where was she? Could she be safe?

Montross smiled weakly. "Yes, where is she, this darling wife of yours? And how safe? She must be alone. Even if she got out by the secret passage, how safe could a woman heavily pregnant be with a band of lawless brigands on your land?"

Raymond stared at him.

"Oh, yes, I knew about the passage. How do you think I got inside, you dolt? My sweet Allicia found it and of course she told me. She wanted me to come to her. She loved me. Only me. Always me."

Once again Raymond hauled Montross to his feet. "Where is Elizabeth?"

He had seen no sign of her in the passage or the holly bushes—but he had not been looking. Was it possible she had gotten away, in her condition and alone—or was this a lie? Even if Montross were mortally wounded, he was obviously well enough to talk and order his men to take Elizabeth. *"Where is my wife?"*

"I hope you've lost her, Raymond. I pray she is dead, so you will know the hell that I have suffered since you killed my beautiful, passionate Allicia."

His head fell forward.

"Fane? *Fane!*" Raymond cried, raising his voice as much as he could.

It was too late. Fane Montross was dead.

As Raymond let his body slide to the floor, a sob of hopeless despair broke from his lips. Where was his beloved Elizabeth? Was it possible she had escaped? If so, he could find her and all would be well.

Then, as if from far away, he heard the sound of a great crash.

He knew that sound. The battering ram had broken through.

His grip on his sword tightened as Raymond ran from the room. He stopped at Cadmus's body and looked at the nick in the wall.

This was his hall, his home, and that of his dear wife. It was his duty to protect his people, and now, his people needed him.

He couldn't leave. Not yet. He would defeat these brigands, and then he would find her.

Please, God, he must find her, and she must be alive.

Or he might as well die, too.

He continued down the steps. As he reached the hall, he ignored his terrified servants and tenants running toward the kitchen. They could take refuge there, in that smaller room.

But he must rid their home of this vermin.

Raymond took a deep breath, raised his sword over his head and, with a low, wolf-like growl, attacked the armed men coming through the shattered door.

And then those men learned that Lord Kirkheathe's reputation did not rest solely on an intimidating presence and rasping voice.

Chapter Twenty-One

Raymond made straight for the first man he saw. The fellow had barely turned around before Raymond struck him fast and hard, slicing into his arm. His companions stared in stunned silence as, with a bellow, the man grabbed his wound. Then the more quick-witted ones came at Raymond.

Two more fell to the rushes, wounded.

Seeing their captors' attention taken from them, Greta gave a great shout. The women fleeing to the kitchen with her turned as she did, and rushed forward. They tackled the men closest to them, Greta screaming obscenities the whole while and clawing at them like an Amazon, her desperation making her nearly mad. The attackers' swords were knocked from their hands before they could react. They lay on the ground, covering their heads with their hands to ward off the blows rained down upon them by the angry, determined women.

Before Raymond could defeat the final two opponents he faced, a group of his soldiers led by Aiken appeared at the ruined door. Seeing them, Raymond's fatigued foes immediately threw down their weapons in surrender.

"My lord!" Aiken cried in astonishment. "How did you—?"

"Donhallow is retaken?" Raymond interrupted.

Aiken drew himself up. "Aye, my lord. Those blackguards had no stomach for a fight with real soldiers, and your men arrived and routed the last of them. Cowards, the whole lot."

"Good," Raymond said. "Now we must search for my wife."

"Your wife?" Aiken murmured. "Isn't she…?"

"No, she is gone."

"How did she do that? The door to the hall was bolted after I went out. And the kitchen, too."

"The same way I got in, and more than that you may not know, since I swore an oath to my father to keep that secret.

"Take these men to the dungeon, and the rest of them, as well."

Greta came forward. "My lord, I fear…I think…"

"What?" he asked, keeping his voice as level as he could, and regarding the fierce Greta with new respect.

"I think Lady Elizabeth was in labor, my lord."

Raymond felt as if his stomach had plunged into the rushes at his feet.

In labor? She went through the passage in labor, and then far enough away that he had never seen her when he came to Donhallow?

"Find the midwife and bring her here," he said to Greta. "I will have her waiting when I return with Elizabeth."

He would return with her, he silently vowed.

He must return with her. The alternative was too terrible to contemplate, for Montross was right. He would suffer as he had never suffered before if she were dead.

Yet worse even than that, he realized with another wave of sickening fear, would be to never find her at all.

"But my lord—" Hale protested.

Raymond's brows lowered ominously as he turned from looking out into the courtyard to regard Hale and Aiken, standing nearby. "It has stopped raining."

"It's still pitch dark, my lord," Aiken noted quietly, "and the ground will be slick with the rain. The horses may fall and injure themselves or the riders on their backs."

"My wife is out there somewhere, and she must be found," Raymond muttered, his angry tone belying his fear and anguish. They had been forced to abandon the search when the rain turned into a deluge. During that time, he had given orders about the burials, including that of Cadmus, and seen what else needed to be done in the aftermath of the attacks.

But now the rain had stopped. He didn't care that it was hours till dawn. "We'll take torches."

"My lord," Hale said sympathetically. "We're all worried about your lady wife, but we can't risk losing more men. Enough have died today."

Raymond ran his hand through his hair and thought of the men who had perished that day in defense of Donhallow, Barden among them.

Hale was right; he couldn't put more of his men in danger.

"I'll go alone," he said. He would risk Castor to find Elizabeth, but no more. "Send out search parties in the morning."

"I'll go with you, my lord," Hale offered.

Raymond shook his head. "No. I have made you commander of the garrison, so your place is here. You stay, too, Aiken, to see that the people are provided for, especially the wounded. If I am not back in the morning, send out search parties regardless."

Hale looked as if he was about to protest, but wisely, he held his tongue and nodded.

"My lord," Aiken said, "it is dangerous for you, too, and not just from the rain and the dark. There may be more of those outlaws still on our land, and you will be alone."

"As is my wife, so I cannot rest until I find her."

"Very well, my lord," Aiken replied. "Good luck and Godspeed."

"Godspeed, my lord," Hale seconded.

Raymond nodded his farewell, then grabbed a torch from the nearest sconce and marched to the stables where he ordered his horse saddled and made ready. The groom looked askance, but nevertheless obeyed at once.

He would start at the exit of the passage, Raymond decided, and search for any clue that pointed to Elizabeth and the direction she might have gone.

He would find her. He had to find her.

If she had already given birth in the open, and in the rain, it was likely too late for the child. But his wife was young and strong—and his heart simply refused to believe that she could be dead, too. She who had brought light and happiness back into his dead existence could not be gone forever.

"Ready, my lord," the groom murmured.

Raymond handed him the torch, then swung into the saddle. He took the torch back from the groom and headed to the gate, then out into the silent village, the only noise the occasional bark of a dog and the dripping of water from the buildings, the only light the small pool that surrounded him cast by the torch.

It was like purgatory.

Forcing himself to keep Castor to a walk and looking about for any sign of Elizabeth, he rode to the holly bushes. When they reached the holly, he dismounted and searched the branches, paying no heed to the sharp edges of the dark green leaves.

When he was nearly ready to give up and go farther afield, he spied a piece of fabric caught on the tip of a leaf and made a small, harsh cry of triumph as he tore it off.

It was from Elizabeth's dress.

So, she had come this way, and she was headed east.

Taking hold of the horse's reins with his free hand, holding the torch high in the other, he began to walk toward the east, his gaze searching the muddy ground.

If only it hadn't rained! Then he would have more hope of finding footprints or other evidence.

If only he could be certain she had kept going in this direction...

He reached the road. Had she gone along it, looking for help, or, fearing discovery, kept to the woods?

He hesitated, unsure what to do, thinking of her alone and enduring the pangs of childbirth, then bearing the child without any help. He listened, half hoping that he might hear a baby's cry or Elizabeth calling his name.

Nothing.

It was as if he was all alone in the world, as he had been before Elizabeth.

Would she risk the road or the wood?

As he tried to decide, fatigue threatened to overwhelm him.

"Oh, God, show me," he pleaded, his own rasping voice loud in the silence of the night. "I don't know what to do!"

Elizabeth would protect their child with her life, if need be. She would try to stay clear of the outlaws.

She would avoid the road.

Whether these thoughts were divine inspiration or not, they were the best guide he had, and he plunged into the wood.

If only there was a full moon! If only it were day. If only he had stayed with her in Donhallow…

He spotted a small white, sodden mass on the ground.

He couldn't breathe. His heart seemed to slam into his chest as he stared at it. Finally, he forced himself forward.

It wasn't a baby's pale dead body. It was a piece of cloth that had fallen over a branch.

He bent down and picked it up, examining it in the torchlight.

Elizabeth's scarf! He recognized the mend in the corner. His knees went weak with relief.

"Thank God," he murmured fervently. "Thank you, God, for this sign."

With renewed vigor he went forward, scanning the ground, seeking other evidence of Elizabeth's passage. The torchlight was not nearly bright enough, but he would not give up. Not when he was sure she had come this way.

He was nearly at the fence before he saw the cottage.

He raised the torch higher. There was no light from the small building, and the only sound was a grunt from the pigsty.

He stuck the torch in the soft ground, looped his horse's reins over the fence and, hiking up his tunic, climbed over it. He retrieved the torch and went toward the cottage.

The windows were shuttered. It might be deserted, the tenants gone to the castle for safety.

Nevertheless, Elizabeth could have sought shelter here, he thought with growing hope. He went to the door and pushed it open.

His heart leaped. She was there, lying motionless on a rough bed of straw in the corner.

Then he saw the blood.

And realized how pale her face was.

Dear God in heaven, she was dead.

He dropped the torch onto the packed earth at his feet and sank to his knees as great sobs of despair and desolation broke from his lips, his whole body shaking with the force of his anguish.

She was dead. His reason for living was dead.

"Raymond?"

With a gasp at the sound of his whispered name, he tore his hands from his tear-streaked face and stared, to see Elizabeth's shining eyes watching him. "You're alive," she whispered as a tear slipped down her pale cheek.

Weak with relief as well as exhaustion, she smiled as he rose.

Her husband, her love, tall, imposing in the darkness, was safe and well, praise God! And so was the child she held nestled in her arms.

"I knew Montross couldn't defeat you," she murmured as he knelt beside her. She managed a smile. "You will wake our son with that noise."

He looked down in wonderment as Elizabeth moved her torn garment that she had used to swaddle their baby away from his little face. She had tried to clean him as best she could. As if annoyed at being disturbed, the babe screwed up his face and started to cry lustily. "Our fine son."

"Our son," Raymond repeated incredulously.

Gathering them both in his arms, he sobbed not with sorrow, but with unbridled joy.

Elizabeth wept, too, even as she laughed. "You will crush him, my love. He looks to be a strong child, but not as mighty as that."

Wiping his cheeks and obviously struggling to get control of his feelings, Raymond drew back—but only a little.

"But how…?"

"The usual way."

"Alone?"

"Do you see anybody else, my lord?" she asked with another tender smile.

She would spare him the details of his son's birth, of her pain and fear, the dread that there might be something wrong, until the baby came, crying before she could even pick him up and wearily marvel at the perfection of his fingers and toes.

"Oh, God, Elizabeth, my Elizabeth," Raymond murmured as he kissed her forehead. "That you were alone—"

She put a finger to his lips. "It is over and I am well, and the babe is, too. Not that I would wish to repeat this."

"No, never." Raymond's concerned gaze swept over her. "Are you naked?"

"My clothes were soaked through from the rain. I had to take them off," she explained as she put the baby to her breast. He latched onto her nipple and sucked, while Raymond sat back on his heels and marveled.

"I thought I was hardy."

"No doubt my years in the convent prepared me."

Raymond looked as if he had been taken ill. "There is so much blood. Are you certain all is well?"

She followed his gaze to the blood-soaked straw upon which she lay. "There is always blood at a birth, Raymond. You have seen blood before, I think. Indeed," she said, her brow furrowing, "you have some on you now."

"Montross and some of his mercenaries are dead."

"Good."

"But so is Barden, and a few of our men."

Tears filled Elizabeth's eyes. "I'm so sorry."

"I think it is well for Montross that Cadmus killed him, for surely he would be hung for a traitor otherwise."

"Cadmus killed him?"

Raymond nodded. "And he killed Cadmus."

"Oh, Raymond, I made him stay, to give me time to get away."

"As sorry as I am for his death, it is worse that so many good men died for Montross's villainy, and it would have been a thousand times worse if Montross had found you, Elizabeth."

"Raymond," she said as the tears fell down her cheeks, "I want to go home."

"Yes, of course. At once," he replied, rising. "I have brought a horse."

"I don't think I can ride."

He rubbed his forehead, trying to think.

"Perhaps the farmer has a cart?"

"Yes, yes, of course. I'll go and see. The sooner we are all safely home, the better."

"We are already safe," she whispered as she watched him leave. "Now that you have come."

A few weeks later, Elizabeth stood on the threshold of their bedchamber, a large wicker basket in her hands. She watched her husband as he leaned over the oaken cradle and cooed to Brennon, their son. He had recently returned from Chesney, where he had gone to explain to the earl what had happened, and to deliver the mercenaries they had captured for judgment.

The earl had been justifiably outraged when he heard of Montross's attack, that emotion no doubt increased by the knowledge that when Montross moved against Raymond, he had gone against a man who now had significant allies. They could have accused the earl of failing to control his vassal, and that would have made things very difficult for him.

Since Montross had no heirs, the earl had given Raymond his estate. Raymond had decided to make Aiken the steward, a worthy reward for Aiken's actions during the attack, as well as his faithful service for several years.

"I thought you were going to let him sleep this time."

Raymond straightened abruptly, his expression sheepish. "He's still asleep."

"Good. I don't want him to wake for a little," she said, gripping the basket tighter as she came into the room.

"Johannes told me they can hear him crying in the village. I hope he's only teasing me. You know, my love, Brennon is a little young for a harp, even the small one you have asked Johannes to make." She sat on the chair she used when she nursed Brennon, the basket on her lap.

"Perhaps I have been hasty. It's only..."

"What?"

"I've been thinking that perhaps, when he grows to be a man, he will sound as I used to."

"Your voice, you mean?"

He nodded.

"Perhaps, but I like your voice just as it is."

"You do?"

"I do. It's very exciting, actually. The first time I heard you speak, well, it did frighten me, but it was also thrilling."

He looked at her, a mischievous gleam in his dark eyes that was even more exciting than his husky voice. "Truly?"

"Truly."

"I don't think I will ever understand you."

"A man should never understand his wife. Think how boring that would be. A little mystery is a good thing."

"Such as what's in that basket? That's a lot of clean linen, if that's what's inside."

"It's not linen. It's a gift."

"For Brennon?"

"No, my love. For you." She set the basket on the floor. At once, the lid shifted and a black nose appeared.

"A dog?"

Elizabeth laughed at his wary expression. "Well, it's not a snake," she said, pulling off the lid completely to reveal a large brown puppy with one black ear, a huge head and enormous paws. It gave a little yip, jumped from the basket, careered into Raymond's leg, then ran around the room, sniffing until it got to the post of the bed, where it raised its leg.

"Oh, dear," Elizabeth said, rising to fetch a cloth to wipe up the mess.

"Yes, we have quite enough of that with a baby," Raymond remarked, taking the cloth from her. "Let me do that."

"I had a baby, Raymond, not a fatal wound."

"You lost a lot of blood," he said, wiping the floor.

"No more than any woman who gives birth."

Finished, he matter-of-factly tossed the cloth out the window.

"Raymond!"

"What else was I supposed to do with it?" he said as he washed his hands in the basin.

"Wash it!"

"It's got dog urine on it."

"I know that. Good heavens, Brennon won't have a bit of linen left if you do that with his."

"That's different."

"For you. You don't have to wash them."

Raymond turned to her with a wry grin. "Neither do you, my lady."

She pouted very prettily. "Very well, I don't— but I have done my share of washing, Raymond. Besides, you never said what you think of my present."

He raised one brow quizzically. "The one chewing on my boot?"

She whirled around and saw that he was right. The puppy lay sprawled on the floor, blissfully gnawing one of Raymond's boots. "Oh, no!"

Her husband came up behind her and wrapped his arms about her, tugging her gently back against his chest. He kissed the side of her neck. "It's an old boot."

"Do you like my present?" she murmured as pleasurable thrills tingled along her body.

"Very much. I couldn't have selected better myself. How did you come to chose him?"

"He's the biggest, ugliest puppy I could find."

Raymond turned her around to face him.

"Well, it's true, and it wasn't easy. Most puppies are very sweet and cuddly."

He curled his lip. "I wouldn't want a sweet and cuddly dog."

"That's what I thought."

"You are a bold, saucy wench," he growled.

Seeing the laughter lurking in his eyes, she pertly replied, "Which is why you love me."

His smile warmed her as much as his embrace. "You are right, Elizabeth. I love you with all my heart."

"And all your body? I am quite healed, Raymond, and the midwife says that we can..." She wiggled her brows suggestively.

"Now?"

"Brennon should sleep a while yet. I fed him but a short time ago."

Raymond looked over her shoulder. "And young Cadmus the second has fallen asleep in my boot."

She glanced back and laughed softly. "He looks right at home."

"He is, and I am at home, too, more than I have been in a very long time, my love."

"Are you going to keep talking, my lord, or take me to bed?"

He swept her up into his arms and whispered in his low, husky voice, "To bed, my lady. To bed."

* * * * *

Harlequin truly does
make any time special....
This year we are celebrating
weddings in style!

A
Walk
Down
the Aisle

WEDDING CELEBRATION

To help us celebrate, we want you to tell us how wearing the Harlequin wedding gown will make your wedding day special. As the grand prize, Harlequin will offer one lucky bride the chance to **"Walk Down the Aisle" in the Harlequin wedding gown!**

There's more...

For her honeymoon, she and her groom will spend five nights at the **Hyatt Regency Maui.** As part of this five-night honeymoon at the hotel renowned for its romantic attractions, the couple will enjoy a candlelit dinner for two in Swan Court, a sunset sail on the hotel's catamaran, and duet spa treatments.

MAUI
the Magic Isles™
Maui • Molokai • Lanai

To enter, please write, in, 250 words or less, how wearing the Harlequin wedding gown will make your wedding day special. The entry will be judged based on its emotionally compelling nature, its originality and creativity, and its sincerity. This contest is open to Canadian and U.S. residents only and to those who are 18 years of age and older. There is no purchase necessary to enter. Void where prohibited. See further contest rules attached. Please send your entry to:

Walk Down the Aisle Contest

In Canada	In U.S.A.
P.O. Box 637	P.O. Box 9076
Fort Erie, Ontario	3010 Walden Ave.
L2A 5X3	Buffalo, NY 14269-9076

You can also enter by visiting www.eHarlequin.com
Win the Harlequin wedding gown and the vacation of a lifetime!
The deadline for entries is October 1, 2001.

HARLEQUIN®
Makes any time special ®

PHWDACONT1

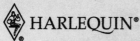

USA Today bestselling author

STELLA CAMERON

and popular American Romance author

MURIEL JENSEN

come together in a special
Harlequin 2-in-1 collection.

Look for

Shadows and *Daddy in Demand*

On sale June 2001

HARLEQUIN®
Makes any time special®

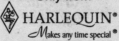

Got a hankerin' for a down home romance?
Pick yourself up a Western from Harlequin Historical

ON SALE MAY 2001

CIMARRON ROSE
by **Nicole Foster**
(New Mexico, 1875)
An embittered hotel owner falls for the beautiful singer
he hires to revive his business.

THE NANNY
by **Judith Stacy**
Book 2 in the Return to Tyler historical miniseries
(Wisconsin, 1840)
A handsome widower finds true love when he hires a
tomboyish young woman to care for his passel of kids.

ON SALE JUNE 2001

THE MARSHAL
AND MRS. O'MALLEY
by **Julianne MacLean**
(Kansas, 1890s))
A widow wishes to avenge her husband's murder, but
soon loses her nerve—and then loses her heart
to Dodge City's new marshal.

Available at your favorite retail outlet.